THE HOLLOW REALMS

MOONLIT SOUL

JORDAN ALLEN

Copyright © 2023 by Jordan Allen

Cover illustration by Lucyan Carreira

Interior illustrations by Theodoric S. Taylor

ISBN 978-1-9196192-8-6

For my beloved family.

Contents

Prologue

Reverend Toulon prayed in front of the statue of the angel. He prayed to the True One that the demons would not make it through the gates. He and the other priests had blessed every inch of the temple, but if the onslaught continued then it would only delay the inevitable.

"They're breaking through the barricades at the bridge, Father," said Pierre the acolyte as he rushed into the hall. His voice trembled with fear when he spoke.

"It was only a matter of time," lamented Reverend Toulon with a heavy sigh and rising to his feet. "Our last line of defence is the walls. Those won't last long with how many of them there are."

"Should I send word to the women and children that they are to make their way down the mountain? It is a treacherous route, Father, but we're left with no other choice. For them to stay here would be certain death for they cannot hope to fight."

Reverend Toulon nodded solemnly. "We are too few and too weak to defeat the entire horde, but we can buy them some time. Let us do what we can for them while we are still able, even if the cost is our very lives."

Pierre clasped his hands together and dropped to his knees. "I...I fear, Father," admitted the acolyte, his voice weak and raspy. "I do not like to admit it, but I must be true."

"What do you fear, Pierre?"

"I fear that we won't be able to buy them enough time to escape. I fear that those wretched demons will desecrate these hallowed halls. I fear all of it."

Reverend Toulon was sympathetic to the young man. His faith in the True One was strong, but he did not have the years and wisdom that Toulon had. "Even if this temple is desecrated, which I have no doubt that it will be, the True One does not die with it. We are one outpost in a hostile world of many faithful. The people who escape will spread the word so that our brothers may be better prepared and fortified against evil. Rest assured that if we act now, we give them the best chance they have. Let us go immediately and linger no further."

"Yes, Father," said Pierre, wiping the sweat from his brow. "You are right, of course. I am sorry for despairing so."

"We all have moments of weakness," said Toulon, "but we push through the fear so that we may persevere with full hearts. Be strong and faithful, Pierre."

The priests walked from the hall and into the courtyard. For centuries, this temple had stood tall above the town of Autun. They surveyed the courtyard for what they knew would be the last time and walked into the centre of the crowd awaiting them.

"Great people of Autun," began Toulon, his voice powerful and commanding. "The demons are fast approaching and there is no way through them. The only option for survivors like yourselves is to take the back route down through the mountains. Trek across the plains to the nearest town and beg them for refuge while warning of the dangers on their doorstep."

One woman chirped up. "But Reverend Toulon, we will not survive the journey down the mountain, never mind the plains. It is half frozen from the cold. We'll break our necks."

"The True One will guide you, my dear lady," smiled the Reverend comfortingly. "The men, the acolytes and I will be staying here to face the demons head-on. If we can buy you an extra hour to make a safe escape, then we have done our jobs well. I do not want to waste your precious time any longer. Follow Acolyte Pierre and he will show you the tunnel to the other side of the mountain. Every male older than thirteen should remain here. Bless you, all."

The families wept together and held each other tightly, knowing they would be torn apart further than they had already been this morning. Men said goodbye to their wives and mothers said goodbye to their sons. The Reverend could not look, knowing that it was his decision. He knew it to be the right decision, but it did not make it easier.

One young lad, no older than fifteen gave a gold ring to his younger sister. "Father gave this to me, and now I'm giving it to you. Treasure it always and do not forget us." The little sister nodded, with silent tears streaming down her distraught face. She wrapped her arms around her brother's waist, refusing to let go of him.

Acolyte Pierre beckoned them all to follow, knowing that time was short. If the demons had broken through the bridge barricades, then it would be minutes before they arrived.

Reverend Toulon addressed the remaining citizens along with his fellow clergy. "Those who are weak and with no magical skills, I want you atop the walls throwing whatever you can get your hands on. The strong, stand ready by the gate to meet the enemy head-on. My fellow priests, bless whatever weapons you can find and be ready to heal whatever wounds are inflicted upon us."

"What about you, Father?" asked a sullen man. "Are you not going to fight with us?"

"My dear friend, I will be front and centre in the courtyard. I will repel the demons that break through the gate. I have no doubt that I will be one of the first to fall. If that is so, then know that I died in service to you."

"What happens when they reach the courtyard?" asked a young lad. He could not have been older than fourteen.

"If you cannot kill them then push them back as best you can. If they break through our ranks, we make for the church hall. Barricade the doors and keep strong. If they break through those too, then make for the roof. We must distract them for as long as humanly possible. If we are faithful enough, the demons may not even realise the women and children are not here before they're already down the mountain. Every second counts."

The crowd dispersed and the men hurriedly took their positions. Priests moved from man to man, casting divine blessings on whatever weapons they could.

"They're here!" called an old man from a corner watchtower.

"I cannot do this," wept a young man barely old enough to grow whiskers on his face. "I cannot do this!" He clutched his sword so tightly his knuckles were as white as snow.

"Hold strong, boy," said Reverend Toulon in a calm, but powerful voice. "The True One will see us through this, one way or another. Have faith and remember why we are here."

"Yes, Father," said the young man, his lip quivering.

"No mercy for them!" roared Reverend Toulon to the men as a wave of fireballs was lobbed over the walls.

The men atop the walls shouted vigorously and tossed objects of all sorts at the enemy below. Planks of wood, loose bricks, even their own boots. The demons took little notice for they were armed to the teeth with plate, chain and shields and their thick demon flesh.

Suddenly the door was ripped from its hinges and a burly demon with two large claws and heavier armour than the others led the charge towards the townsfolk. It broke through the line of men effortlessly and tore many in two with a single strike.

Reverend Toulon cast the divine Push spell, a prayer to the True One that sent a shockwave of energy from his palms. The clawed demon was knocked back. It yelled in a hideous language that no man present would even want to decipher, lest their flesh melt from their bones.

It had been less than a minute and half of the remaining men retreated to the church and closed the door, leaving the rest of their comrades to face the demons. They were outnumbered by the infernal hellspawn.

The clergy brought a few of the demons down while the Reverend himself continued to battle the clawed demon, but he was running out of spells to repel the beast. He took another tactic and cast the Great Barrier spell, forming a wall of energy around himself.

Toulon charged at the demon and his spiritual wall knocked the demon to the ground. He cast True Touch and grabbed the demon's claws with his bare hands. The sharp blade-like nails cut into his palms, but the demon was in pain for the first time.

The brute kicked the priest off and leapt to its feet. Toulon fell backwards and his barrier dissipated. The demon jumped at the priest, who threw it backwards with his Push spell, and the demon's head smacked the stone with a gruesome crack.

The brave priest rose up and quickly glanced at his surroundings. It was a bloodbath, with the townsfolk losing badly. The fathers were cut down, the sons were incapacitated; some pitifully begged for their lives, accepting the forever bargain that demon's presented. Join them and become one of them.

Try as he might to resist, Toulon was in despair; he was a mere mortal, after all. He prayed to the True One as his opponent stood back up then reformed his holy barrier, protecting himself once more. He charged at the demon who was forced back again and plunged his thumb into the demon's eye.

The demon howled in anguish as its eye was burned by the magical touch of Reverend Toulon. Suddenly, the priest felt a sharp pain in his back as another demon joined the battle and had torn Toulon's lower back open with a grim battleaxe.

He sank to his knees as the howling demon with the brutal claws, now one eye lesser, approached him. The priest's chest heaved up and down as he tried to catch his breath and whisper a final prayer to the True One. The infuriated demon raised its arm high and swung his claw through the air, separating the priest's head from his body, and casting his unsullied soul to the Inner World.

Chapter 1

The Escapist

The moon hung low in the sky, peeking out from behind the barren mountains at the prison by the river. It had been a long night for the assassin as he waited in his cell within this fortress that he was forced to call home for the time being. He had given up on cursing and grumbling, for it had not helped his mood one bit. Not that he had expected it to.

The usual unpleasant snorts and harsh shouts from the vile demons that had imprisoned him could be heard echoing through the corridors of the prison tower where Tarn sat. They were louder than usual, perhaps they were bickering over which prisoner would be tortured next. Most who were dragged off returned brutalised or in pieces and were then left to die in agony before their various parts were dumped into the river outside. Those who were kept alive were only allowed to live so that the torture could continue. A great humiliation, for the demons did not seek any knowledge that the humans may have to offer, for their arrogance in their own false civilisation was so great.

Tarn put his face close to the barred door and tried to catch a glimpse of whatever the commotion was. All he could see was the dark brickwork that was tinted a yellowish-orange by the glow of the lamplight. Seeing nothing remotely interesting, he returned to patiently sitting by the barred window where the steel rods were even more tightly fitted than those of the door. He stared at the small fraction of the moon that he could see. Tarn had always marvelled at its beauty and longed for the day that the Queen would descend from it. Oh, what a glorious day it would be.

He quietly sang a song to himself as he watched the dark clouds roll along the night sky. It had been two days and nobody from the Order of the Blood Moon had come for him. If he had been a higher-ranked member, he would have been freed within twelve hours. It must have been because nobody had noticed he was missing yet. Yes, that was it. He conjured a tiny flame on his tongue and blew it out the window, letting it dissipate into the night. He continued doing this in silence to pass the time, a minor amusement in a sea of boredom.

"Back to the hells with you!" yelled a husky voice from a nearby corridor. A cacophony of demonic screams and screeches followed.

Something was afoot.

Tarn returned to the door, listening intently to the grunts and squelches that echoed down the corridor. He could hear the sharp clink of metal growing louder and louder. Whoever that voice belonged to was coming this way at a brisk pace.

Suddenly, a man in heavy plate armour ran past the bars before doing a double take upon seeing a prisoner present. The man stood in front of Tarn; his face was obscured by a grilled helmet with a red feather plume trailing out from the top. The assassin could see a pair of shadowed eyes staring at him through the narrow slits. This knight wore a blue cloak that was lined with grey fur and Tarn could tell the man would be a formidable opponent for whatever unfortunate demon would cross his path. He had a strong air about him, one that said he feared no foe, demon or otherwise.

"Get out of here," said the man as he hurriedly unlocked the door with an unseen key. "There are more of them coming, but if you stick to the shadows, you may stand a chance. You cannot come with me for I go further into the bowels of this wretched place."

Tarn did not say a word as the man ran deeper into the prison tower, precisely the opposite of what Tarn planned to do once he had retrieved his belongings. He pushed the barred door open with a faint smile on his face and stepped into the corridor. He listened and could indeed hear more demons coming this way.

The assassin could see that the corridor before him was narrow enough that if he were to lie down his head and feet would touch both walls. It adorned with low archways that were engraved with lion heads, perfect for cover if one were an insect nesting in the crevices. The walls themselves were dry and rough, not too slippery. The perfect texture for what he planned to do next.

Tarn ran in the direction of the commotion and effortlessly stepped on the walls, before leaping towards an archway overhead. He grabbed an inch-wide outcropping with his fingertips and swung himself sideways. He quickly placed his hands and his feet on opposite walls and held firmly. He waited, suspended ten feet above the ground, staring downwards.

Sweat dripped from his forehead as the horned demons in their black armour ran past, chasing the man in the blue cloak. Tarn was not tired, he was nervous. Getting caught here without weapons would not end well for him and he knew it. To his great relief, the demons did not notice him hiding in the darkness overhead. They clanked and grunted away, fading into a slight echo.

Tarn waited a few more seconds until he was certain the coast was clear, then dropped to the ground, landing nimbly on his feet. He ran in the direction the demons had come from, stopping at every corner to make sure more weren't guarding their posts. No, most had indeed been distracted by the heavily armoured intruder running through their halls.

He couldn't help but notice that all of the cells he had passed were empty. Perhaps he was the last prisoner? The man in the cloak hadn't stopped to release anybody else. No doubt, Tarn was next on the list to be tortured and the timing of his release could not have been better. As handy as his fire trick was, it was much more useful for lighting torches than setting his enemies ablaze.

There, a window without bars. Tarn entered a side room, a small dormitory for guards, and opened the window. He leapt onto the ledge and lowered himself from it, gripping tightly. He was safe for now, hanging onto the edge of the tower dozens of feet above the ground. Not a place that many would feel comfortable, but the people of the Blood Moon could think of nowhere they'd rather hide.

The assassin looked around, trying to find the easiest way to the base of the tower. He had little knowledge of this place but would have bet good money on his mask and ring being stored in the chamber at the bottom. He knew it was a good bet in theory, but he had the lingering fear that the demons had already claimed his possession for themselves and were tainting them with their filth. Perhaps they had already destroyed them, fearing the return of the Queen. No, it was best to push those thoughts out of his head.

Tarn let go and fell fifteen feet, before gripping onto the next window ledge. He did it again, and again, then one more time. He looked over his shoulder and could see a walkway a short distance out from the tower. If he fell, he would break something. If he landed, the demon slowly walking up the walkway may see him.

With no time to waste, the assassin pushed himself from the tower and threw himself across the gap. He rolled upon landing, then hurled himself over the battlement, hanging on tightly. By some miracle, the demon had not spotted him. It continued its patrol, blissfully unaware of anything amiss in the castle.

"Stupid beast," thought Tarn to himself. He had no respect for demons and their ungracious ways. They had no loyalty; they had no ideals. They were mere beings of spite, jealousy and anger. The only thing they had left in common with humans was hierarchy. With a gathering of demons this large, that meant that there was a more powerful demon nearby to lead them. All the more reason for him to escape. Tarn was not deluded enough to believe that he could cleanse this place if he tried, nor did he have any desire to. It was a job for others, he had a more important task.

The patrolling demon walked by Tarn, who climbed up quietly and crept up behind it. He grabbed the demon's sword and jammed it inside its helmet, producing a gruesome squelch. Tarn ripped the blade out and kicked the demon aside. The demon fell with a metallic thud, as Tarn sped off. He kept low, wanting his presence to go unnoticed for as long as he could muster.

Halfway along the walkway, he found a staircase leading into a small courtyard where the tower entrance sat on his right. On his left was an archway, leading towards the main, much larger, courtyard near the entrance. He needed to go this way once he retrieved his gear. He ran to the tower door and hastily opened it.

Whatever trouble his saviour was causing for the demons right now was to Tarn's great benefit. The room was unattended. He ran down a small corridor and into the chamber he was seeking. All of the castles, forts and citadels in this land bore striking similarities. He knew them well from his past life, rather than previous imprisonments. He rummaged through the crates and trunks that lay before him.

"There," he muttered to himself. "You are as beautiful as I remember, whether red as blood or white as the soul."

Tarn slipped on a ring made of a dark grey metal. Within the ring was a blood-red crystal, glistening even in the low light. The light in the crystal swirled and rotated, holding secrets that only the Order of the Blood Moon were privy to. He caressed it gently, knowing that it was priceless.

Next, Tarn placed a black, wooden mask on his face. It was filled with ornate golden etchings and shaped perfectly for his face, custom-made by a fine Rochian craftsman. All that was still visible of the assassin's visage were his eyes and lower jaw. This mask was him and he was this mask. Without it, he was a common man. He was nothing.

He could not find his weapons or armour, but he would worry about that later. If he could escape, he could get new weapons and armour at the nearest shrine. He had his most important belongings, and his priority was to escape and find out where his target had retreated to.

Tarn had been tasked with the killing of a demon hunter named Sir Chaville, but he was waylaid by a patrol of demons. Had he known that this place, Ouvergarde Castle, had been taken by demons then he would have avoided this route. It had been an intended shortcut but, alas, he would get back on the trail before too long. He had no other choice.

The assassin ran from the room and back to the courtyard, making for the archway underneath the walkway he had crossed minutes ago. Wearing his mask, ring and wielding the demon's ugly longsword, he felt considerably less vulnerable. Frankly, he would have felt the same even without the sword.

Tarn could see the wooden doors up ahead across the much larger courtyard. To no surprise, they were closed. Demons stood guarding them and even more demons filled the courtyard. They had not been drawn away by the intruder for whatever reason, but Tarn knew that he was close enough that he could escape. He could taste the freedom that lay beyond the gates. He just had to make the right moves and he would be out of here in minutes.

He hid in the shadows cast by the nearby outbuildings. He examined the courtyard, safely concealed in the cloak of darkness. There were nine demons in total between him and the doors. If he could get past them, he could make for an opening to the left of the gate.

He was certain it would lead to a staircase, then the main battlements of the castle. It was at least a thirty-foot drop at the other side, but it was a drop he knew he could survive if he was careful. Possibly even with both ankles remaining unbroken, which would have been most welcome.

Tarn waited for all of the demons to face away from his direction, then slipped inside the building. It would be difficult for a normal man to see anything, but Tarn's enchanted mask let him see in the absence of light. A magical power that came in very handy in his line of work. Darkness was both his greatest ally and his enemies' greatest foe.

Inside the building was a small kitchen and a

collection of bloodstained beds, the inhabitants long gone. The assassin raided the room, looking for anything that could provide a good distraction. He grabbed a few rotten tomatoes and two kitchen knives that had seen sharper days. He slipped out of the building and back into its shadow.

Tarn put a foot on an outer window ledge and jumped high in the air. He pulled himself onto the roof and lay flat on his stomach. There were more guards on the battlements, so he had little time before he was spotted.

Tarn hurled a tomato at the nearest guard in the courtyard. It splattered on its armour with a squelch, leaving a glistening stain. The demon knight growled something in an indecipherable language to his ally. When they glanced in the direction of the building, Tarn dropped another tomato from the roof.

The guards ran over, with swords drawn, to investigate. When they had wandered into the shadows, the assassin quietly descended from the roof. He crept up behind and slit the throat of one of the demon knights.

As the other demon began to cry out for reinforcements, Tarn shoved his sword into the back of its throat before it had the chance to raise the alarm. Both demons fell to the ground with a thud. Two less problems to deal with, that would have to do. The short journey to the opening in the wall would be that much easier.

Tarn removed the armour from one of the demons and hastily donned it. He knew he would be uncovered as soon as the others noticed he did not have the large horns the demons possessed, but it may get him far enough that he can run past his patrolling foes before they're fully aware of the human imposter.

The disguised assassin walked across the courtyard. Within seconds, a demon pointed at him and yelled its warbling gibberish. He had hoped that he would remain undetected for a few seconds longer. All of the demons turned towards Tarn, who sprinted forwards, making a beeline for the small doorway.

As one demon approached, Tarn hurled one of the blunt knives into the opening of its helmet. It collapsed on the stone floor as Tarn was accosted by another demon. It stabbed at him, but even in the cumbersome armour, he was too fast for it. The assassin parried with his looted sword and kicked the demon to the ground. He continued to the gate and through the small doorway as the demons chased.

Tarn threw off the helmet as he ran up the circular stairs. A demon from the battlements burst down the staircase, eager to meet him. The demon slashed downwards, but Tarn stabbed it in the hand with the remaining kitchen knife. It winced in pain but did not scream. Tarn grabbed it by the arm and tugged, pulling it down the stairs. As it tumbled, he charged up towards the battlements.

He reached the top where one more demon waited for him already as others ran in his direction with murderous intent. He was mere feet away from escaping this place. He would not fail now. Tarn duelled the raging demon, trying to end the fight quickly.

The two traded blows, but Tarn got the upper hand. He knocked the demon's blade from its grip, then stabbed it in the leg, where its armour could not protect it. He grabbed the demon and threw it down the stairs, hoping to buy a few seconds of time.

Tarn hurriedly abandoned the rest of the armour and ran to the edge of the battlements. The path towards the mountains stretched out before him, but something more pressing caught his eye.

A large, hunched demon was staring up at him from below. It had limbs like an ape, but where there would normally be hair there were scales. It had the burly head of a bull, but its horns were twisted and splintered like the branches of a tree. It had a large tail that forked towards the end, each branch a large blade sharp enough to cleave stone in two.

Tarn could hear the demons approaching from behind. He had no time left to waste. He raised his blade and jumped at the demon guarding the gate below. It roared at the man leaping towards it.

The assassin jammed the blade into its skull. The beast howled in agony, as Tarn landed on the ground. It was a rough landing, but he was unharmed. The beast continued to scream, but the assassin did not have time to fight it. He knew he would die if he tried.

He climbed to his feet and sprinted down the road. He did not look back until he was safely behind a large rock at the foot of the mountain. The guardian did not leave its post, enraged as it may have been nor did the demons within the castle emerge from the gate.

Tarn breathed a sigh of relief and fell onto his back. He stared at the beautiful moon, and she stared back at him lovingly. He held up his hand

and gazed into his ring, the swirling red enchanting him as it ever did.

"Soon, my Queen," he whispered.

Chapter 2

A Sentinel's Job

"Back to the hells with you!" yelled the man in the silvery plate armour, striking at the demon knights with his claymore.

The demons screamed and screeched as they were cut to pieces by the Outer Sentinel. The fabled paladin would see this castle burned to the ground before allowing a single one of them to dwell here past tonight.

Chaville ran down the corridor, his metal armour clinking and clanking against the stone floor of the prison tower. He stopped and walked backwards, staring into the cell. A pale man with dark hair and a faint scar on his lip stared back.

"Get out of here," said the Sentinel as he held

his hand to the door and willed it to unlock. The lock clicked from his magic, freeing the prisoner. "There are more of them coming, but if you stick to the shadows, you may stand a chance. You cannot come with me for I go deeper into the bowels of this wretched place."

Sadly, Chaville could not help the man further. He must reach Za'grudeaux before more demons arrive. Being outnumbered against a powerful foe like the possessed lord would be most unwise.

The man said nothing as Chaville ran further into the corridor. The poor fellow was probably malnourished and tortured by the demons. Who knows how long he had been trapped in the cell with only the moonlight to keep him company?

The staircase lay just ahead. The burly Sentinel skipped most of the steps as he hurried down. He burst through the door at the bottom and into one of the castle courtyards where the keep awaited him.

The night was chilly, but he barely noticed. The mighty warrior had demonic bloodlust to keep him warm. By his hand, Ouvergarde Castle would be set free. His armour glistened in the moonlight, peeking out from behind the mountains.

Two demonic knights wielding halberds stood tall, guarding the keep door. Chaville held his blade tight and focused on a prayer. His blade began to glow a white light, enchanted by his Holy Steel spell.

The knights separated as Chaville approached, moving to flank him. The Sentinel was unconcerned by such meagre demons, whatever their advantage may have been.

"Come at me, you vile savages," he taunted,

beckoning them forwards. One of the demons took the bait and thrust his halberd at the paladin. Chaville readily swept it aside with his claymore.

The second demon slashed at him, while the first spun around to deal a follow-up blow. Chaville managed to ward off the first blow but took the second slash to the arm. His plate armour protected him, but it left a small rip in his cloak.

Infuriated by his favourite blue cloak being torn, Chaville cast a Push spell, knocking the demon knight to the ground by an invisible force. He focused on the one still standing and cut its polearm in two when it made for him again.

The demon charged in for a tackle, but Chaville thrust his blade forward. The metal cut deep into the knight's shoulder, where the magic took effect. The wound glowed brightly as the demon roared in pain, the holy magic of the True One igniting his infernal blood and killing him from within.

As the demon fell to the ground, the other arose. It ran at Chaville, the tip of its halberd aimed directly at his throat, but the Sentinel was too quick. He batted it aside and cut the demon's head clean off.

It smacked the ground as the holy warrior made for the gates. He glanced over his shoulder and could see more demons emerging from the prison tower. He opened the doors forcefully and slammed them behind himself.

Chaville looked towards the far end of the room, where a man sat on the throne. Well, it may have once been a man, but it was now a different beast entirely.

The former Lord Grudeaux sat on his chair, possessed by the demon from the hellish plane of

Za, Za'yithka. He was adorned in intricately patterned, copper-coloured armour, wearing a helmet with a long red plume at the top back. The helmet grill was lowered and two demonic horns had erupted from the helmet.

The overtaken lord had renamed himself Za'grudeaux, which alerted the Outer Sentinels. The demons in their desire to brand their targets, whether by blade or by name, was an unsubtle tactic.

Chaville looked at his target and pointed his blade at the imposter. "Your foul acts have not gone unnoticed, Za'grudeaux. The punishment for your unholy crimes is death. I, Chaville of the Outer Sentinels, will see that you die tonight. Do you have any last words?"

Za'grudeaux laughed coldly. "You are a fool to have come here, paladin. We are peaceful demons, merely minding our own business, and you invade my castle? You threaten me with death inside my own keep? Your ill manners are most unbecoming and I demand that you leave at once."

"I will not play these games with you," barked Chaville. "Contain these poisonous lies and mockeries within your mouth. You have invaded the Outer World and possessed a respected Lord of Roch, a protector of these lands. This is not your keep and you will be removed by force, there can be no peace between us."

Za'grudeaux let out an exaggerated sigh and stood up. He clenched his fist tightly, then unleashed it. A ghostly longsword of red light spawned in the demon lord's hand. The very sight of it was pure evil and made the hairs on the back of Chaville's neck stand up.

The demon lord walked down the staircase, swinging the blade, ready for a fight. "I will give you one chance to join me, paladin. A capable warrior like yourself would be a fine asset to the demon army of Za. The power you could wield with infernal blood and sorcery would surpass all you could do with your divine magic."

"Never," spat Chaville. "Have at you!"

Za'grudeaux ran forwards and the two warriors clashed. The holy magic of the claymore collided with the infernal body of the longsword. When one sword struck the other, a heavy rumbling burst out. Each, trying to shatter the other.

The man and the demon exchanged blows, neither faltering. Chaville blocked and parried while Za'grudeaux thrust and slashed, trying to find an opening in the Sentinel's defence.

Chaville swept aside a particularly powerful strike and cast the Push spell on Za'grudeaux's leg, knocking the demon lord off balance. He hacked at the demon and it fell to the ground. As Chaville raised his blade for the kill, the demon lord rolled aside and clambered to its feet.

The demon raised its arm high and three magic circles drew themselves on the floor. Three scraggly whelp demons appeared, looking like malnourished peasants, and darted for the paladin. He cut each down as Za'grudeaux leapt at him, using the whelps as cover.

The foolish lord had left himself open and Chaville thrust his sword forward, skewering the demon through the throat. The holy magic from the enchanted blade sent ripples of light through the demon's body.

Chaville forced his blade further inwards,

placed his foot on Za'grudeaux's armour and forced the demon lord backwards. The possessed lord's blood spilt across the stone floor as its infernal weapon dissipated.

A cloud of black smoke burst from the lord's open neck wound. A green-skinned demon collapsed to the ground, frail and pathetic.

"You win, paladin," croaked the demon, climbing to its feet. "Allow me to return to Za."

"For your crimes," said Chaville, raising his blade, "the punishment is death."

The paladin beheaded the scrawny demon in a swift motion, and it collapsed to the ground in a wretched heap. Chaville sighed and dragged the body of Lord Grudeaux to his throne. He doused the body in oil from his pack and retrieved a torch from the wall.

Saying a silent prayer, the Sentinel cut the horns from the deceased lord's body and set him alight, entombed within his noble armour. Chaville, paladin of the Outer Sentinels, departed from the keep, seeking to cleanse the leaderless demons from Ouvergarde Castle. He was far from finished.

He strode down the stairs, greeting the demons that met him in the courtyard with a swift end. As the demons fell, Chaville made his way from room to room, slaughtering the invaders. He ascended every tower and he scoured every corner. No demon was safe from the wrath of the Sentinel.

He did not see the man he had freed from the cell, so perhaps he had already escaped. It was truly Chaville's hope that the man was free, for nobody deserved the fate of being a demon's prisoner. Death or joining them were often the only options, but joining them meant the death of the soul.

The paladin dealt with the last of the demons atop the battlements and gazed over the gate at the larger demon he knew awaited him. The Gate Guardian. He knew that if he survived his short stay within the walls, he would have to face it if he wanted to return to the road.

Its bull-like head stared up at him, its apish limbs were long and dangly and the horns on its head looked empty without a half dozen bodies impaled upon them. Chaville had avoided this beast before, knowing that angering it would alert the entire courtyard. Granted, he did that anyway when he scaled the wall and landed in front of a demon knight on the battlements. Stealth was not the paladin's strong suit, especially when covered in heavy armour.

"Most curious," muttered Chaville to himself, his gaze fixed upon the Gate Guardian's head. "I don't recall seeing that before."

There was a crude blade sticking out from the beast's head, but it was still standing strong. Where the blade came from, he could only guess, but each guess was as wild as the next as they flickered through his mind. He cast them aside, knowing that it did not matter much. Perhaps a second impalement to the skull, a holy one, would be enough to finish the beast off.

Chaville recast his Holy Steel spell, filling his claymore with divine might once more. He leapt from the battlements with the large blade poised to pierce the scaly flesh of the Gate Guardian. It stared at him intently as he descended through the air, its mouth dripping with saliva and with every intent on devouring the tasty morsel that was delivering himself to it.

The demon suddenly swung its body round, whipping its forked and bladed tail at the paladin as he plummeted. Chaville was knocked aside, landing clumsily on the ground as the demon whipped back around and made to grab him with its hideous palm.

He hurried to his feet, narrowly avoiding the demon's mighty claw. He retrieved his sword and stood ready, as the brute swung a large fist at him. Slashing at its knuckles, the beast roared as the divine energy seeped into its infernal blood. A creature this large would not be felled easily, even with the magic of the True One infesting its very being.

Chaville readied himself as the creature swung its tail once more. The paladin thrust his claymore into the ground, held the handle tight and threw himself upwards. The beast flung its tail straight into the blade and it was sliced in two as Chaville flew clear.

As the Gate Guardian recoiled, Chaville landed on his feet. He pulled his sword from the earth and charged forth towards the demon. He raised his sword high and cut its stomach open, spilling its miserable guts onto the dirt path. It collapsed to the ground in a heap, alive, but defeated and in excruciating pain.

The paladin said a short prayer as he stood before the beast which made a fruitless attempt to right itself. "Whoever you once were, I hope that your soul will find peace now. May the True One bring you home one day." He cut the Gate Guardian's throat and it finally succumbed, dropping to the ground which shook under its immense weight.

This job was over and Ouvergarde Castle was cleansed of the demon scourge. There was not much time to rest however, there never was. It was time to move along to the next job that Chaville was tasked with completing.

A horde of demons had ransacked the town of Autun and claimed a Temple of the True One as their own, desecrating it and turning it into a debased Temple of Mallabeth. It was an affront unlike any other, a truly wicked act that even some of the most devout mortal cultists would not dare. Not necessarily out of respect, but because they knew the consequences would be dire.

One of the town's former residents, a man named Chatou the Bard, had sent word to the Outer Sentinels and Chaville had agreed to the job. If he had not, it would not have been done with the Sentinels being as stretched thin as they were. Autun was a couple of days ride to the north, but it was a journey worth making. At least the sights along the way would be pleasant to the eye before he reached the town, and everything turned sour.

The paladin hoped that Chatou was still alive and well. Sometimes those who provide the Sentinels with intelligence get tired of waiting and get themselves into a whole heap of bother. It was hard to blame them when the Outer Sentinels could take weeks, if not months, to answer the call in these trying times. It was unfortunate, but Chaville was doing all he could and carrying more than his fair share of the work.

He walked down the road towards the rougher terrain. There was a small clearing that he had found where he had tied up his horse, Avalanche, who was faithfully waiting for his master's return. Had a demon dared to come for the stallion, it would have found itself with a hoof-shaved hole in its head. A truly loyal steed was Avalanche, one who had been with the paladin through thick and thin.

Chaville walked up to his palomino horse and stroked his mane. "You're still here, I see. I thought you had perhaps grown tired of our demon-hunting ways, Avalanche. Did you not follow your dreams of chasing wild mares across the western plains?"

Avalanche let out a soft whinny which Chaville guffawed at. The horse could always unwittingly keep his spirits high. He reached into the horse's pack and pulled out a handful of oats to feed him. Avalanche eagerly licked them up and munched down.

"No? The reward for our work is worth it to you then?" asked Chaville, patting Avalanche's side. "We'll stop a little way up the river where you can have a long, uninterrupted drink. You have earned that for your eternal patience. Would you like that, my friend?"

The paladin chuckled as he let the horse finish his snack. He retrieved a waterskin and took a swig, before hoisting himself onto the horse's back. The last few hours had passed quickly in the heat of the battles, yet it also felt like days since he arrived at the castle. A feeling all too familiar to him.

"You know where we're going, right?" asked Chaville, stroking his horse's mane.

Avalanche answered with a deep neigh, and

Chaville tightened his grip on the reins.

"Then let us go," ordered the paladin.

The horse broke into a gallop and the duo rode off into the night, making their way north.

Chapter 3

The Queen's Favour

The sun was rising, obscured by the clouds and the mist that had captured the land this damp morning. Had it not been for the early daybreak, it would not have been obvious that Spring was here in the Kingdom of Roch.

It was a kingdom known for its harsh terrain and even harsher denizens. Rochians were a hardened and proud people, made even prouder by the many hellish demon invasions they had suffered in recent years. With every attack, they persevered.

Had it not been for his orders, Tarn would have refused to kill a man like Chaville. Perhaps it was fate intervening that led to his imprisonment, perhaps it was simply horrible luck, but he was free now and had to see his task through.

Chaville was a member of the Outer Sentinels, but that was all that Tarn knew about his target. The Outer Sentinels were demon hunters in the service of the True One, the supreme god of the Inner World. A realm that lay deep within this hollow world where all resided. The lands that lay on the surface were known as the Outer World and between the two worlds lay the hells, the source of the demons.

Tarn had travelled through the mountainous terrain for a couple of days, reaching the pine forest where the nearest Blood Moon shrine was hidden. It was here that he would be able to locate his target once more and resume the hunt. All he needed is two other members of the Blood Moon to assist him.

Tarn climbed a small hill where three tall standing stones sat. Each was inscribed with a rune. The first translated to blood, the second to soul, and the third to vessel. All three stood in the clear, where the moonlight may shine upon them in the night.

The assassin kneeled down in the centre point between the three stones and touched his ring to the ground. He breathed deeply, then spoke the words that would let him be truly hidden once more. "In the name of the Moonlight Queen, welcome me home, as I will welcome her home."

He closed his eyes and when he reopened them, he was no longer atop the hill. He was now within the hill, where no passer-by could hope to reach him. The Order had many of these hideouts scattered across the kingdom and beyond, from Lochmeria to Kalmere, there was not a nation that had been left untouched by the hand of the Blood Moons.

The main chamber was lit by glowing white moonstones. In the centre of the chamber stood a statue of a woman. She was tall, beautiful and elegant. Her hair was braided and she wore a flowing gown, so sleek that you would not realise that it was made of stone. She clutched her hands to her chest, where they rested holding a crystal.

Tarn kneeled at her feet, kissed them. He begged for forgiveness for his recent capture, then arose and sang a soft song.

> We seeketh blood and soul
> To fill the crystal urn
> Both guilty men and innocent
> For release, they shall yearn
>
> We will make their end swift
> Neither painful nor cruel
> For they are all the keys
> At the time of the renewal
>
> When the advent draws near
> No more essence shall we glean
> They will gather in red moonlight
> For the arrival of our Queen

The Song of the Blood Moon was a song that all of the assassins knew. It signified their dedication to her cause. Whoever they targeted was inconsequential to them. Friend or foe, stranger or family; it did not matter. It was a choice that each member had already made when they chose to pledge allegiance to the Moonlight Queen. The consequence for betraying the pledge was death.

When he had finished, Tarn walked down the tunnel that the statue of the Moonlight Queen faced. He had not been to this shrine before, but they all had similarities. He followed the tunnels to the armoury and tore off the wretched garments that he had worn during his short stay in the prison. He chose out a finer cloth and adorned his black leather armour, along with a dark, hooded cloak.

Once he had found a suitable dagger and short sword, he walked back to the main chamber and squatted down before a small pool of water. He removed his mask and rinsed his face. He dried it with his sleeve and placed his mask back on.

"You have failed," came a woman's voice from behind.

"I have not failed," said Tarn, without turning around. "I have been waylaid. It is only a failure if either my target dies or I die."

"You can dress it up however you please, but a better assassin wouldn't have gotten captured. You lost track of your bounty and his soul continues to wander freely in its fleshy shell. You have failed."

"You knew that I had been imprisoned, yet you did nothing?" asked Tarn, turning around.

The woman standing before him wore similar attire to Tarn, however, her mask differed. It was a mask that was painted purely gold and the face was patterned like a butterfly. Too flashy for Tarn's tastes and certainly not making for an easier stealth-based approach. He recognised this woman from a previous unpleasant encounter, she was called Joiselle.

Joiselle was not alone. Beside her stood a bulky

man in black leather armour, but Tarn did not recognise him. His mask was as black as his armour, shaped like the top half of a skull and ending with a row of teeth. Tarn wondered if they were real teeth as they glistened in the light differently from the rest of the mask.

"Why would we intervene?" asked Joiselle. "You are a lowly man with only a half-dozen retrievals to your name. Your target was a member of the Outer Sentinels and would surely kill you first, should you have encountered him. I don't see how it would be worth the effort."

The bulky man spoke in a low voice. "Yes. You were deemed not worth the risk."

What an insult. "What happened to brotherhood between assassins?" asked Tarn.

"We prioritise."

"Who are you?"

"Guion," the man said simply, clearly not looking for a drawn-out conversation.

"I would apologise to you both, and all other assassins, had I indeed failed. As I have not, I will expect an apology from both of you when I succeed. And mark my words, I will succeed."

"I wish you the best of luck," said Joiselle sarcastically, doing an exaggerated bow.

"In spite of what she says, I do wish you luck," said Guion, sounding somewhat earnest. "Your target is difficult and you lack the skills to kill him. Do not take that personally, as there are many others who would struggle equally."

"It is clear that both of you think little of me," said Tarn, "but I have a favour to ask, Blood Moon to Blood Moon. I would ask others if they were here, but we are alone in the shrine."

Joiselle looked to Guion, but he did not react. She turned to Tarn and let out a small laugh. "Fine. Let us hear it."

"I need to perform another scrying ritual. I am not prepared to let Chaville get too far before I track him down. The sooner, the better."

Guion slowly nodded. "I will agree to that."

"I will not," said Joiselle. "You lost your target; you can track him yourself. I will not aid incompetence."

"You will respect the bond between the Order of the Blood Moon members," demanded Tarn, raising his voice. "By the Queen, you will pay if your insolence continues. Once you assist me, I will take my leave and we need not lay eyes on each again."

Joiselle was shaking with anger. Guion placed a hand on her shoulder, trying to calm the enraged woman. "Fine," she begrudgingly said.

Tarn stood in front of the statue of the Moonlight Queen, Joiselle to his left and Guion to his right. All three were evenly spaced in a circle around the figure of their goddess. Tarn held his hands together and began to chant a song in a language known only to the Blood Moons.

His ring started to shine brightly, then Joiselle and Guion joined in the song. Their rings glowed brightly, both with swirling white rings that contrasted to Tarn's red. It was an extra humiliation for Tarn knowing that they had recently completed a hunt while he was in the shrine with an active hunt.

Suddenly, after the seventh repetition of the song, Tarn's eyes glowed blood-red from behind his mask and he hovered off the floor, rising to meet the face of the Moonlight Queen statue. Her crystal began to glow and Tarn was no longer in his own body.

A man was riding on a palomino horse down a road. The horse trotted along at a brisk pace, but in no major rush. Out of the right corner of the man's eye, there was a pine forest. On the road ahead, a mountain, many miles in the distance. Tarn tried to take the details in, but suddenly the vision was broken.

Tarn dropped to his feet, back to seeing through his own eyes once more. "Where?" he asked, sensing he was deliberately pulled from his trance by one of the others.

Joiselle shrugged her shoulders, but Guion turned to Tarn. "I have walked this road before. It leads to a town called Autun. It was ransacked a few months ago by demons worshipping Mallabeth. I do not know if any are left alive, so you should stay off the beaten path where you can."

Tarn nodded. "Thank you, Guion. The man is a demon hunter, so it stands to reason that he's trying to take the town back from the infernal plague of hellspawn."

Joiselle scoffed. "That is a bold assumption. He could be a scout for all you know."

Tarn raised his voice again. "It may be bold, but I would bet my mask that it is correct. I shall leave once I have consulted the maps. Guion, do you know how far the journey is?"

Guion folded his arms and nodded his head. "He is a few miles ahead of you, but I would say it's two days on the road. If you cut through the pine forest then you may be able to make it before him, even without a horse. The town is sitting in a valley between two sides of the mountain, you will know it when you reach it."

"I had better leave immediately," said Tarn.

"If we do not lay eyes upon each other again, I will presume you are dead or captured," smirked Joiselle.

"You will meet the grave before I do, I assure you."

"I hope that isn't a threat, Tarn. You know the punishment for killing another member of the Order of the Blood Moon."

"It was not a threat, but an observation of your lack of skill. You have been guided by luck which will run out quickly."

Joiselle was shaking once more. "You had better leave before your target escapes once more. I wouldn't want you to fail again."

Tarn thanked Guion for the information and rushed to the study to find a map of the area. He grabbed a small pack, stashed his rather limited supplies and used his ring to depart the shrine the same way he entered.

*

The forest was thick with fog, making it hard for Tarn to navigate the hills and thickets. A far harsher route than the road the demon slayer had taken, but Guion was right. It would certainly be faster braving the forest as long as the assassin didn't break his neck along the way.

Roch was divided into two extremes, rough badlands of stone and high-altitude forests and mountains where the cold would devour you without shelter. Had it been three months ago, Tarn would have been frozen solid.

He trod carefully along the mossy cliffside path, making sure to keep his eyes to the ground rather than towards the moon. It was difficult for him, enamoured by its splendour as he was, but he kept himself in check. There could be no more room for error if he were to prove Joiselle wrong. More importantly, he must prove to the Queen that he is her more dutiful servant.

Suddenly, there was a crunching of leaves nearby. The assassin leapt onto the wall of the cliff and pulled himself upwards and out of the way of any predators that may cross his path. He readied one of his throwing daggers, should an unfortunate beast wander underneath his position.

He listened intently for a few minutes, but nothing crossed his line of sight. Perhaps it was a particularly fat squirrel looking for food now that winter had come to an end. He did not believe that for a second but knew that he had to push on. Tarn lowered himself back down softly and continued forwards more slowly than before.

Another crunch. There was something nearby and it knew that he was here. He jumped from the cliff and onto one of the trees that sat just below the edge. He could not see the ground below, but surely nothing would dare try its luck reaching him from here.

Suddenly, the tree began to violently shake. Who was below and what did they want? It would take a giant to swing a tree as sturdy as this so vigorously. The assassin leapt over to the cliff and climbed back onto the path he started on.

The tree had stopped moving. Tarn leaned over the edge of the cliff and tried to see the forest floor, but even with the magical power of his mask that let him see in the dark, he was unable to see through solid objects. The branches and leaves were simply too wild and too thick.

This would not do. Tarn was the hunter, not the prey. He would deal with this troublemaker and get back on track afterwards. He climbed down the rough cliff to the forest floor, his sword at the ready. He looked around but could not see anything. Stone, trees and lots of tangled foliage littered the ground.

Tarn fell to the ground as a thick branch smacked his back. He rolled forwards and back to his feet, thrusting his sword in the direction of his attacker. He struck the air with no attacker to be found. Whoever was there was toying with him.

The branch ahead drew itself back and swung at the assassin. He ducked low, avoiding the attack, but he was so taken aback by the tree moving of its own accord that he did not even notice the vines wrapping themselves around his ankles.

"Show yourself," he demanded. "Whatever mage powers you're using to control nature, whatever sorcery you use to disguise yourself, you are nothing more than a coward. Show yourself and face me."

He tried to step backwards and tripped. From the ground he could hear the crunching once again, then he saw a faint green glow emerge from one of the trees. A creature with bark skin approached him, followed by another and then another. They stood and smiled with their carved faces as another vine wrapped itself around Tarn's neck.

The assassin tried to wrestle free, but it was tightening around his neck and choking him. He tried to cut the vines, but they were too thick. As he struggled, more wrapped around his arms and held him down. He was completely subdued and the sylvans began to close in on him.

Chapter 4

To the North

Chaville rode into the quiet town as the sun began to fall behind the mountains. Only a few stragglers were still on the streets at this hour, something that would be most unusual only a few years ago. The watchmen were already roaming the town with their swords by their sides and lanterns in hand, but they had yet to light them.

"Who are you, traveller?" asked one of the watchmen as Chaville trotted along the street towards the inn. The watchman had his hand on the hilt of his blade.

"My name is Chaville," said the paladin. "I'm with the Outer Sentinels. I seek a place to rest for the night." Chaville had been questioned by two previous watchmen and had patiently answered their questions. It was understandable that they were so cautious in troubling times.

"You would not mind if I asked you to raise your grill, Sir Chaville?"

The paladin complied and revealed his face to the guard. "I am a pure-blooded human, I assure you. I serve only the True One and no others from the mortal realm nor the hells beneath us. If there is anything else I can do to prove this to you, I will do it."

"That won't be necessary," said the watchman, relaxing and letting go of the hilt of his sword. "I'm sorry to have troubled you. I trust that you have pressing matters, as you lot often do, but can I ask a favour?"

"Most certainly. If it is within my power, I will do it."

"If there is trouble in the town throughout the night, can we count on you to fight alongside us and help keep the people here safe?"

"It would be an honour to serve your town, diligent watchman."

"Thank you. If you're looking for a place to rest, Greymane's up ahead has rooms." The guard pointed up the street to exactly where Chaville had been heading. The paladin politely thanked him and took his leave.

He tied Avalanche up outside and walked into the small establishment. He tossed the innkeeper a couple of silvers for a place in the stables and a room for the night. An envoy from the Outer Sentinels was due to meet him here this evening, so Chaville waited in the near-empty inn.

"It's quiet," said Chaville to the innkeeper after

sitting silently for a short while.

"That it is, sir, that it is. The townsfolk are all at home with their doors locked, and you don't get many travellers on the road when demons surround your town to both the north and the south."

"The south has been cleared; I assure you. I intend to deal with the north once I'm rested."

"Sir, I admire you and your folks, but the whole world is being attacked by the hells. Demon attacks are more and more common in Roch and beyond. There's a reason they have you doing two jobs rather than two Sentinels taking a job each."

Chaville nodded. "It is true that we are being stretched thin, but we are still mighty and we are still winning. The hard times will pass and there will be peace once more."

"I wish I had your faith," said the innkeeper, rubbing his neck awkwardly. "I truly wish you the best of luck, sir."

The paladin sat quietly in the inn and waited. What the innkeeper said was true. Demon attacks had become more and more common. The world was growing darker and the Outer Sentinels could not train new members fast enough, even when the Saints themselves urged the people to join the ranks.

Whatever was enticing the demons as of late, Chaville did not know. Perhaps it was a co-ordinated attack from the various hell realms? Perhaps just an unfortunate coincidence? The reason mattered less than the response and Chaville insisted on righteous fury against the invaders.

Eventually, the door to the inn opened and a

young man entered. He wore dull steel armour and a blue tabard over it, bearing an angelic being. Images of the True One were forbidden, so the Outer Sentinels tended to use angels to represent their faith.

Chaville stood up and gave a salute. "It is good to see you, Sir Florian."

The young man kneeled before his superior. "Likewise, Sir Chaville. I trust that you are well?"

"Arise and be at ease," said Chaville, and both men sat down. "I am fatigued, but well. It is nothing that food and rest won't fix."

Chaville called to the innkeeper who brought over a few rolls of bread and some cooked, but now cold, mutton. The two men prayed together, then ate up the basic meal quickly and quietly. Both were starving from their long day and rations were even less satisfying than this disappointing meal.

"What news do you bring about Autun?" asked Chaville, once both men had finished eating.

"Our scouts have followed up on Chatou the Bard's information. The town has indeed been overrun. We cannot easily reach the desecrated temple in the mountain above, but everything else has been verified. We have no reason to doubt what he says."

"What types of demons are we dealing with?"

Florian scratched his chin. "A few of the typical sorts, from whelps to soldiers, all seemingly demons from Kee. There's one demon we've happened across that's particularly of note. We call him the Fat Demon."

"I take it that he's very large in girth?" asked Chaville, holding his hands out wide.

"That is a fair assessment," laughed Florian.

"He's as tall as a house and wide as one too. His boils look to be filled with acid and he wields a giant bone club. His stomping can be heard from halfway across town so if you don't see him, you'll hear him."

"Any good tactical entry points?".

"Approach up the mountain path from the south, but avoid the pine forest. It's not good terrain on horseback, even though it's a much quicker route, and there are even rumours of sylvans within the northern forest. Word is that there are also Blood Moons who have taken up residence somewhere in the southern part of the forest. They probably won't cause much trouble, but if you get too close to their shrine, they may pose a problem."

"I'll stick to the main road. It doesn't sound worth the hassle for all of a few hours difference."

"You will be a day slower, perhaps. There are tunnels through one of the other mountains that may save you an additional couple of hours and guarantee you arrive in daylight, should you not wish to waste time camping an extra night. I know little of them, so tread with caution if you take this path."

"If the town is overrun and the people are either dead, gone or demons, then I do not think a day will matter much. Daylight is important, as you know."

"Yes," agreed Florian, "those were my thoughts as well. It will be a challenge, even for a Sentinel as capable as yourself, but I'm confident that you can handle these demons."

"Very good," said Chaville. "If you pass over whatever documents you've brought, I will study up tonight and hit the road at first light."

Florian reached into a sack and handed Chaville a small roll of papers. The paladin had a quick glance at them, noting the orders, the tactical assessment and surveying the map briefly.

"It all looks to be in order," said Chaville. "Are you returning to base or are there more deliveries to make?"

"I have one more a few towns over," said Florian. He looked tired. "I don't think there's a single soul in the church who isn't worked to the bone. Priests healing and blessing, scouts riding the lands, and the paladins like yourself on the hunt. I will travel through the night and see how far I get. No rest for men like us, eh?"

"Indeed," said Chaville standing up. "I'll bid you farewell then, my friend. Thank you for coming all this way."

"You're welcome, Sir Chaville," said Florian, also climbing to his feet. "Thank you for the meal. I will pray to the True One that he may watch over you on this mission."

"Safe travels, Sir Florian."

Florian departed and Chaville retreated to the room he had rented. He poured over the documents, studying the routes to the town, Autun's layout and the run-down on each of the demon types that had been spotted. The Outer Sentinels were nothing if not thorough. Chaville had always told his comrades that if they did not study ahead of a job, they would have a much harder time. The ones who listened usually came back alive.

Demon species were not entirely consistent, but they were often predictable in their aggression.

Chaville had spent nearly two decades fighting them and was one of the most respected men in the Outer Sentinels for his capabilities. He had lost count of his kills when he reached a thousand, but he was well on his way to having five thousand dead demons to his name.

It was almost midnight by the time the paladin slept. The maps were engraved in his mind and he was looking forward to the hunt when he reached his destination. He always did.

*

Chaville awoke at the crack of dawn, guzzled down a hearty breakfast of beef and potatoes, a more satisfying meal than the night before, then departed from the inn. He had decided that he would take the shortcut through the tunnels so he could finish the job faster. Poor Chatou the Bard had been waiting some time for his town to be set free.

Avalanche trotted along the path in the misty morning. The sun was starting to creep through the clouds and the day ahead looked promising. Many Outer Sentinels complained about the long hours on the road and not enough hours vanquishing foes, but Chaville enjoyed taking in the sights. Even a simple field was pleasant to him.

"Come on, lad," he said to Avalanche, tugging on his steed's reins. "We're heading off-path now."

The paladin led his horse onto the grass and towards a small valley. A doe stood by the dark entrance to the tunnel nuzzling at its injured fawn.

Chaville dismounted, retrieved an apple from his pack and held it visibly. He then softly approached with his empty hand raised.

The deer looked at him, terrified of something. As soon as Chaville got within ten feet, it bolted in the opposite direction. Chaville squatted beside the dying fawn and inspected a giant bloody patch of its fur. Something had taken a large bite out of the poor fawn. The perpetrator's jaw was wide and its teeth were sharp. It was definitely not human, but the paladin suspected it was not a mere animal.

He sniffed the wound as he raised his hands to heal the deer. It smelled ever-so-slightly of sulphur. It smelled of one of the hell realms. The attacker was a demon.

A soft warm glow emerged from Chaville's hands as he felt a prayer to the True One rush through his body and flow into the young deer. The fawn's wounds began to stitch themselves back together, but it may have been too late to save it. It had lost a lot of blood.

Chaville waited with the little one for a while, encouraging it to take a bite of the apple, but it was dead minutes later. He glanced to his left and could see the mother doe watching him, not daring to approach. He wanted to give her the chance to mourn for her child. He set the remainder of the apple beside the dead fawn and led Avalanche by the reins closer to the tunnel entrance.

He knew it would cost him some time but he could not let this lie. He tied Avalanche up outside the tunnel mouth and walked inside alone. Once he had butchered whatever fiend lay inside, he would return for his horse, but not a moment sooner. A more loyal steed he could not wish for and he could not put his companion in grave danger unless absolutely necessary.

Chaville cast the Orb of Light spell and a small ball of energy floated around him, emanating a warm glow. He walked away from daylight and into the foreboding darkness ahead. He held his claymore in both hands, waiting for any sign of movement.

The tunnel was narrow and winding, twisting like a serpent wrapping around its prey. The dripping of water echoed through the dark tunnels, breaking the silence every so often. The stone walls were slick with moisture and the air was filled with the musty smell of decay. There had been no shortage of death in this dark place. Coming here would have been a mistake for any normal man.

The paladin stopped and listened. There was something more than dripping. A scratching sound reached his ears. It sounded like fingernails on stone. He sniffed the air and could make out the faint sulphuric smell amidst the damp.

Suddenly, a fierce beast leapt at him from behind a stalagmite. The paladin was knocked to the ground and the beast tried to bite at his armour with its huge jaws. The demon looked to be somewhere between man and canine, but bulkier than either. It had no skin to speak of, a being of bone, muscle and infernal blood. Where it should have had two eyes, it had empty sockets leading to nothing.

Chaville threw the blind beast off and climbed to his feet. It turned towards him and snarled, showing off its gaping maw lined with sharp teeth. It leapt at him, but he thrust his claymore forward and it swallowed the blade. Its back burst open as the tip of the sword pierced it, killing it instantly.

Chaville knelt beside it and inspected it as he had the fawn. This was most certainly the young deer's killer. The size of the teeth and the mouth matched. He rose and turned to leave, but as he did so a groaning voice called out.

"Don't go, please..." it said from the darkness ahead. "We have need of you and we are most desperate."

"Who goes there?" asked Chaville forcefully, readying his blade once more. His work here was not done here yet. A strange voice in the darkness never brought good news.

"I am Vachel...at least I used to be. Come closer so that you can see us. You can bear witness to the horror that has unfolded in this unholy place."

"Vachel, ask him to kill us," whispered a quieter voice.

"I will," Vachel whispered back. "Be patient. He is a stranger and we cannot scare away another. Surely, you remember what happened last time?"

"He can end our pain," said a third voice.

"I know that," whispered Vachel as Chaville grew evermore tense. His hands gripped his sword tightly, ready to attack at a moment's notice.

"You are a good man, stranger," said a fourth voice. "I can tell just by looking at you. Please help us."

Very soon many more voices joined in the whispering. They began to chant in unison, asking for Chaville to kill them, but he could still not see their faces. He took a few steps forwards, kicking the dead demon out of the way. He ignored the pathways on either side of him and stepped into a small opening ahead.

The orb lit the cavern and Chaville's eyes widened in horror at what lay before him. There were people here if they could still be called that. At least a dozen of them. Each of them was a mixture of flesh and stone, merged with the wall. Some had only their head remaining while others had most of their upper body free. They were a living mural, stripped of all mobility and bound to the tunnels. An agonising fate.

Chaville drew a holy symbol with his hands across his chest. "I...I am lost for words," he said. "I am so sorry that this has happened to you. I...I am sorry."

The voices all lamented their fate and continued to beg Chaville to kill him, but one of the men in the wall remained silent.

"Which of you is Vachel?" asked Chaville, suspecting he knew already.

"I am," said the central figure who had remained quiet, moving his one remaining flesh hand to point to his face. Even the fleshy hand had a couple of petrified fingers. It wouldn't be long until that too was rendered immobile.

Chaville stood in front of the man with a look of sorrow on his face. "You say you want me to kill you and I will grant your request if that is truly your desire, but I must first ask you two very important questions. I hope you can answer them and I hope you can answer them quickly."

"I will if I can," groaned Vachel, struggling to open his stony jaw. The other mural men whispered uneasily, wary that they would scare off yet another who might end their unrelenting suffering.

"Who did this to you and where are they?" asked Chaville, his voice filled with righteous fury. "I swear to you all that I will make them pay for this."

Chapter 5

Mother of the Trees

"You should not have come here, human," said one of the sylvans with glee as it reached for Tarn's sword. Its wooden body moved smoothly as though it was flesh. It was unsettling to look at.

"A foolish mistake, fleshling," said a second sylvan as the first took the assassin's sword and dagger from his restrained hands.

"We shall bring you to our mother and she will decide your fate," said a third as it reached for the vines. "She will be most pleased with us. Won't she, brothers?"

"Yes," said the first. "We will be her favourite children once we hand over the masked man."

The vines decoupled from the forest floor, but remained tightly bound around Tarn's neck and limbs. The sylvans began leading him forward like an animal. Their wooden faces were filled with glee.

Guion. He had directed Tarn here on purpose. He must have known that the tree spirits resided in the forest and would try to capture him. Another humiliation for Tarn that would surely see him either dead or demoted should he escape and his failure become known.

No, it was not a failure. He would escape once more and deal with this act of betrayal harshly. He was not going to die here and he was going to retrieve Chaville's soul for the Moonlight Queen.

"Walk," demanded a sylvan as Tarn slowed his pace.

"The bonds are too tight, tree spirit," said Tarn. "I am not as adept as you are at moving through these fabled woods as I am a being of flesh, blood and bone. I am not blessed with your wondrous capabilities."

"Your tricks will not work on us, human," chuckled another sylvan. "We know of your kind and what you do. You wear the painted wood of our brother or sister on your face. A mask made from the corpse of our kin and you expect mercy from us?"

"If it is any consolation, this mask was carved from a tree that fell in a violent storm," lied the assassin. "I have the utmost respect for your ways and solely wish to travel peacefully through your forest."

"You would disrespect us by thinking that we are foolish enough to fall for a tongue that speaks only lies? Your poisonous words will not work."

"I assure you that I do not lie to you. I will speak

with your mother, no doubt an esteemed spirit of good judgement. She will understand."

The three sylvans all laughed wicked laughs and continued to pull Tarn along. Other spirits emerged from their trees to watch the captured human be paraded through the forest. Some of them were twice as large as Tarn, others as small as children. A few looked almost like humans, yet others looked much more bestial.

The sylvans led Tarn into a small clearing where a particularly tall tree awaited them at the centre of a pool of green water. Its roots were especially thick and the pine needles particularly sharp.

"Dearest mother," said the spirits in unison, "we bring you a trespasser from the human lands. We found him walking along the cliff to the south. We offer him to you and hope it pleases you so."

The tree's large branches began to stir and the face of an old woman materialised in the wood. Its eyes slowly opened, revealing a deep green glow.

"Human?" said a creaky, echoing woman's voice as the tree's face moved. "What are you doing in this forest? It is not for you, fleshling. It is a home for the trees and the wildlife we permit."

"I am merely passing through," said Tarn. "If you shall allow it, I will depart and never return. I have an important matter to address elsewhere and do not seek to harm you or interfere with your lives."

The tree croaked a laugh. "If one of my children were to walk through your front door, trample all over your kitchen, then ask to go out the back door would you allow it?"

"If it would get rid of them faster, most certainly," said Tarn earnestly.

"Children, do you believe him?"

"No, Tree Mother," they said in unison.

"They are not convinced," said the Tree Mother. "Nor am I. A man who hides his face behind a corpse is surely a vengeful man. He would kill anybody who wronged him for even the slightest matter."

"As wise as you are, Tree Mother, I answered you truthfully. I do not wear a mask so that I can take lives, I wear a mask so that I can save one."

The spirits murmured angrily, but the Tree Mother waved her branches to silence them. "Silence, children. I permit him to continue."

"I roam the lands looking for a way to bring my queen back to life. My brothers and sisters do the same. We are the sylvans and she is our Tree Mother. We love her as your children love you. She loves us as you love your children."

The Tree Mother looked at the sylvans lining the clearing, then at each of the three holding the vines binding Tarn. "It is true that I love my children and that they love me. If what you say is sincere, then I sympathise with your plight."

The tree spirits began to murmur once more. They all looked as doubtful as trees could look, if trees could look doubtful.

Tarn ignored them and addressed the Tree Mother again. "If you allow my hands to be set free, I will show you. Your children have my weapons and I am no spellcaster. Surround me should you wish."

The sylvans all began to yell angrily, then the three tightened their grips. "We will not fall for your deceit, fleshling," said one of them.

"We will grind your bones and fertilise the soil,"

cackled another one of the sylvans.

"Silence!" ordered the Tree Mother. "You will be good children and speak when spoken to. Release his arms, but tighten the grip on his neck and legs. Do it now!"

The spirits complied, as faithful children often do. One of them shot a particularly menacing look at Tarn and the vine around his neck contracted. He was struggling to breathe, but he held up his blood-red ring and waved his other hand over it.

The ring glowed brightly and red lights danced through the forest clearing as the enchanted crystal sparkled. The sylvans were enamoured by the mysterious lights. The Tree Mother herself gazed at the ring in awe until the light began to fade.

Tarn spoke as the vines loosened ever so slightly. "This ring contains a rare medicine that I gather for my queen. That is what you witnessed before you. When I gather enough, she will be restored to life and grace us with her presence once more. It is the water that gives her life."

The Tree Mother's face bore a distraught expression, tears of pine resin escaping her glowing eyes. "It is a gift beyond comprehension for a child to care so deeply about a mother that he cannot move past his loss. My child, you must learn to accept her death."

Tarn was affronted by such a vile comment, but he restrained himself from reacting. "Dearest Tree Mother, I must at least try. You are wiser than I, yet I cannot heed your wisdom for I love my queen so. Will you permit me to bow before you, fully restrained if my intent is still of concern."

"You may," she said as her tears glistened in the

moonlight above.

The sylvans bound Tarn's hands once more and led him forwards to the Tree Mother. He knelt down low, bowing his head to the soil. He had one chance at this and could not miss his opportunity. The Tree Mother would pay for what she said about the Moonlight Queen.

Tarn brought his head back up and stared into the Tree Mother's eyes and breathed as deeply as his restraints would allow. He mustered his rage and blew a small jet of fire straight onto her tears. It was a stronger spell than he had ever cast before, fuelled by fury.

The Tree Mother screamed as the resin caught fire and quickly spread to her bark. She was old and her wood was dry, desperately clinging to the moisture of the pool, but it was not enough to save her. She was dying and she knew it.

The sylvans stared in shock and their vines fell loose, so disturbed were they. Tarn ran straight towards the fire and they dared not chase, fearing the increasingly intense flames that grew stronger with each passing second. The Tree Mother's horrible, agonised screams echoed throughout the night, but her children were too afraid to approach.

"This is the difference between you and I," called Tarn to the spirits. "I will defend my Queen with my last breath, yet you recoil at the very thought of a little heat."

"Spare us!" begged one of the sylvans who had restrained Tarn. The fearful spirit stepped backwards, slowly trying to create a bigger gap between itself and Tarn.

One of the sylvans swung a vine at Tarn, but he

caught it with his hand and pulled it hard, jerking the spirit into the Tree Mother's pool. Tarn stepped forward and grabbed the sylvan by his trunk neck.

The assassin dragged him towards the burning Tree Mother whose screams had faded out, replaced with the crackling of the burning wood. Tarn thrust the sylvan's face into the flames and he began to burn too. His siblings all watched, too terrified to approach the menace that they had unwittingly brought to their sacred grotto.

"Flee for your lives," yelled Tarn, releasing the sylvan who writhed on the ground. "Run away from this place and trouble me no more. Should I see any one of you again, I will burn the entire forest down without mercy. Tree or sylvan, nothing will be spared. You have seen my power, know that I can and *will* follow through."

The assassin grabbed a fallen branch and set it alight. He stepped forward and waved it in an arc at the sylvan who held Tarn's sword and dagger. It dropped them before retreating to the edge of the clearing, where his kin watched and waited. They were cowards.

"Begone!" shouted Tarn, but they did not move. He hoped they would not call his bluff.

He retrieved his weapons but stashed them in favour of his burning branch. He ran towards the edge of the clearing and the ring of sylvans finally broke. They fled as he drew near, and he kept on running. He sprinted through the forest, keeping his burning branch held high. Not a single sylvan dared follow him, for they did not want to end up with the same horrific fates that had befallen their beloved mother and brother.

*

Glad to be nearing the edge of the forest and far away from the sylvans, the assassin forced his way up the latest steep incline. He would redeem his name and his standing. The Order would respect him once again and he would personally ensure that the Queen got what she needed. Souls.

For that was the way of the Blood Moon. When a ring turned red, its owner was called upon by the Queen to collect a soul. As the target died, the soul would be drawn into the ring, preventing it from being sent to the Inner World where it may find peace. A fate worse than death, an endless limbo until the monarch claimed the soul for herself.

Chaville was to be hunted, his name only known because of the first scrying ritual. Tarn had gotten lucky and performed the ritual while the Outer Sentinel had a meeting with one of his superiors about his next task. Had it been any other time he would have had a notably harder time finding him; not that he did find him in the end anyway.

Tarn reached the top of the hill, his legs burning. He scanned the landscape, hoping to see a landmark of sorts. He knew he was close, he could taste the scent of ruin. "There," he muttered, spying the edge of a rooftop creeping out from behind the grey stone of the mountain. At last, he was here.

The assassin pushed forward with renewed strength, convinced that he had beaten his quarry to the town. All he needed to do was find a place to lie low while he waited. This section of the pine forest was quiet, but too far from the road. It had to be in the town. There would be good cover inside the buildings. A simple dagger tossed from a rooftop would be enough to finish this damned mission.

Tarn had spent most of the night in a giddy state, having gotten both revenge for the Moonlight Queen and foiled Guion's plan to kill him. He was certain that the news of the Tree Mother's death would reach the Blood Moon shrine before long if it had not done so already. The traitor would know that Tarn would not be out of his way so easily. The cherry on top was that Joiselle would hear about it and seethe until she bled.

As Autun came more clearly into view, Tarn could see that it was a dishevelled wreck. It had only been months since it was overrun, but the demons had not been kind to it. Not that that was any surprise. Demons loathed humans for the humanity that they themselves had lost. They were resentful, spiteful mutants that had allowed themselves to be cursed with infernal blood. They would never know peace.

Each building that Tarn passed was a haunted shell, bereaved of its family who had cared for it over the years. The stone street was littered with abandoned carts, smashed crates and the half-devoured remains of the people. Disgusting. It was a real shame to see what had become of an otherwise pleasant town in Roch.

Tarn squatted down by the skeletal remains of a young woman, who had already been long dead. She was wearing once-fine garments and an amulet. Inside the amulet was a sketch of her and a young man, standing side by side. Her husband, perhaps? Her fate would be lost with time and there would be nobody left to remember her even a few decades from now. Sad, but that was to be the fate of most of the inhabitants of the Outer World. Only a select few would achieve true greatness.

Tarn heard a thunderous stomping around the corner ahead and dove into an alleyway. He stared at the wall of the building beside him. It was a misty morning and the stone was a little damp, but it should still be scalable.

The assassin leapt onto the wall and grabbed loose bricks to pull himself up. Where there was a crevice, even if only small enough for a finger, he would use that to pull himself further. It was effortless for a man of the Blood Moon.

He climbed onto the roof tiles and stayed low. They rattled as he moved, so he made sure to move softly. He hid behind the ridge and peered over, waiting for whatever was approaching.

As the loud steps grew closer, a huge beast wandered around the corner. It was as tall as the building, and almost as wide. It bore a smile that would shatter any mirror that dared capture its visage. Two small horns erupted from its forehead and three more from each temple.

It was covered in sores and boils, filled with blood and pus that looked like it would melt through stone. It walked on two large legs, muscular and fat in equal measure. Strong legs were needed to carry such a heavy brute. Over its shoulder, it carried a giant bone large enough to have been the leg of a dead giant.

The Fat Demon let out a deep grunt and scratched its behind roughly, snorting as it did so. The ugly beast walked through the street continuing its patrol, unaware of the man who looked on in disgust hidden just out of sight.

Chapter 6

Punishment

Chaville stood in front of the mural men and waited, but none of the petrified souls answered him. "I asked you who did this and where to find them."

"It is too dangerous for you," groaned Vachel. "Kill us and begone from this place, I beg of you. Do not join us upon the wall. It is a fate worse than death. We hunger so, but our stomachs are made of stone. We thirst, but we have no bodies that will be quenched."

"I do not doubt the danger," said Chaville. "I am an Outer Sentinel and will see to it that divine justice is dealt. Was this a demon or an evildoer of mortal nature?" He did not want to believe humans would do this to their own, but he had seen the wretched depths to which some would stoop.

"Tell him about Pilier," whispered another mural man.

"We cannot," said Vachel. "Do not mention him again."

"Perhaps he can avenge us?" asked another.

"Do not speak out of turn," whispered Vachel. "The less he knows, the better."

"Who is this Pilier? Did he do this to you?" demanded Chaville.

"You should not know, for you will go to your grave," insisted Vachel.

Chaville had had enough of Vachel's dodging. "Tell me or I will simply leave. You can remain part of the cave wall for the rest of time, unable to move an inch."

Vachel sighed and finally gave a straight answer. "Yes. Pilier is a mage who calls himself a geomancer. A weak man physically, but sinister and cunning. If he sees you coming, you will end up on the wall with us."

"Then I will ensure that he doesn't see me coming. Tell me where to go. If you do that, I will return and kill you. You have my word."

The mural men looked at each other and all nodded except for Vachel. "Very well," he said. "You smell the scent of death in this place? Where it is strongest, you will find Pilier. He performs wicked experiments on humans, animals and demons. Some of them alive and others dead. He turns them into statues, he turns them into golems and he does...this." Vachel's remaining free arm gestured towards the men embedded in the wall.

"I will not be long," said Chaville as he turned away from the unmoving mural men. He sniffed the air and followed the scent of decay mixed with sulphur. He walked for a while through the twisted tunnels and paused once he heard the familiar scratching sound, but this time something was different. It was not nails on stone, it was stone on stone.

Another demon leapt at Chaville from the shadows, colliding into him. This time he was braced and did not topple, but the beast was much heavier. His orb lit the tunnel just enough for him to see why. The same species of blind demon stood in front of him, but this one was made of stone, transformed from its fleshly self into a demonic golem.

Chaville slammed his claymore into the demon. Small shards of stone chipped off its back, but it was not deterred. It leapt at the armoured warrior once more and clung onto his waist. It pulled, trying to bend the steel and crush the paladin within his armour.

He lifted his claymore high and pummelled the hilt into the stone demon's head. He chipped another chunk from the creature. This was the way. He continued chipping away at the beast until it's head shattered. It released its grip on the man and fell to the ground. Not wanting to take any chances, Chaville lifted the stone corpse, now completely inflexible, high and slammed it into the floor, breaking it into a dozen pieces.

"How I wish I had a mace," he muttered as he continued forwards. He walked and cast Holy Steel on his claymore, preparing it for any demons that may still retain some flesh.

The smell of rot grew particularly strong as he entered a cavern. His eyes scanned the grisly scene that lay before him. The floor was covered by the bodies and bones of the fallen, creatures of all kinds. Half were partially stone and the other were broken statues, but Chaville knew instantly that they were once flesh.

The walls of the cavern were adorned with unmoving statues and heaving golems whose eyes followed him as he moved further and further into the room. A chill ran down his spine, but he remained steadfast as he approached a man who waited at the far side of the room.

He was a mage in blue and grey robes that sat atop a stone throne with a stone crown on his head. Pilier, the lord of this evil domain. The man responsible for the cruel punishment that awaited those who crossed his path. Chaville knew he must be quick.

The geomancer rose to his feet, ready to speak, but Chaville quickly drew his dagger and threw it at the mage, planting itself deep in the villain's gut. Pilier screamed in horror as he realised his death was fast approaching.

"Who...who are you?" he asked shakily, as he dropped his staff on the floor and reached for the dagger in his gut.

"I am Sir Chaville, an Outer Sentinel. You will tell me how to restore the mural men and I will guarantee you a much swifter end."

Chaville walked up to Pilier who dropped to the ground, weak from shock and the rapid pace at which he was losing blood. The paladin grabbed him by the robes and hoisted him onto his throne.

Chaville pulled the dagger from Pilier's stomach, who called out in agony.

"It...cannot be done," said Pilier, pressing one hand on his wound to try and stem the bleeding. "They are my masterwork. A piece of art that will stand as long as these tunnels exist. They will be spoken of for centuries. I have made them immortal."

"Easy now," said Chaville as he spotted the man's hand twitching in the direction of his golems. The mage quickly flicked his wrist and the golems stirred, moving in the direction of Chaville.

The paladin hacked off the evil mage's hands and left him to bleed to death. He ran past the golems, outnumbered and outmatched. They were slow, but they would not tire, even with their master dead.

Chaville sprinted through the tunnels and returned to the mural men. "Pilier is dying, if not already dead," he said hurriedly. "I will return with reinforcements to deal with the stone army once I have finished another job, but I will make good on my promise to you all now."

Vachel breathed a sigh of relief. "Thank you, friend," he said as the rest of the mural men nodded in agreement. Chaville moved from head to head and quickly impaled them with his dagger. He saved Vachel for last, who uttered a final thank you before dying.

The paladin ran from the room, but could hear the footsteps of the army of golems growing closer. He followed the winding path back through the tunnels and out into the sunlight once more. He untied Avalanche, climbed atop his steed and galloped away from the tunnels.

*

It was a misty morning across the plains of Roch. As Chaville approached the mountain obscuring Autun, the pine forest lay on his right. He felt as though this was the exact same path as the previous day as the mountain barely looked closer.

In the valley between this mountain and the next, lay the town. It was there that his quarries awaited him, feasting on the remains of civilisation. Motivated by their evil desire to corrupt and claim, they were spurred on by pure hatred and lust for power.

Chaville squinted as he looked at the road ahead. Was somebody approaching him? He was sure of it. There looked to be a woman on the path, shambling towards him and Avalanche. She did not appear to be in a good way as she grew slowly closer.

The Sentinel raised a hand in greeting. "Ho there, wanderer. I wish you no harm and you may freely approach."

The woman stumbled forwards, then collapsed. She lay there, unmoving, sprawled across the dirt.

Chaville dismounted and approached. "Are you alright?" he asked, checking the woman for injuries. She had a few cuts and bruises across her body.

She grunted awkwardly. "Demons...in town...ahead."

"Yes, and I will deal with them in due course.

Lay still and I will heal you. I'm a paladin of the Outer Sentinels and you are safe from harm while I am around."

Chaville raised his hands and placed them over the woman's wounds. He felt his prayer rushing through his body as his hands glowed a soft light. The woman's cuts stitched themselves together and her skin became unblemished. The scent of pine emanated from her.

"Thank you. What is your name, kind stranger?" she asked.

"You are welcome. My name is Sir Chaville. And you, lass?"

The woman sat up and pulled her auburn hair back. "My name is Joiselle and I come from Autun, the town ahead. You said you're an Outer Sentinel? Does that mean that you are here to help?"

Chaville nodded with a smile on his face, but she could not see it as he was obscured by the grill of his helmet. "I am. As I said, I will deal with the demons in due course. You should get yourself to safety, somewhere far away from Autun." He pointed towards the mountain. "It's been quite a while since the town fell, how long have you been trapped here?"

The woman paused to think. "It has been weeks. The demons are everywhere and I had to hide in a cellar. I was very lucky to find dried food and a barrel of water, otherwise I may have died of starvation. I dared to venture out, hoping that things would be quiet, but there were still demons around. I only narrowly escaped." She began to weep and cupped her face in her hands.

Weeks? Something was not right. "Ah, was it the giant demon with the bull's head and bladed tail that attacked you? I've received word that it's the master enforcer in Autun."

The woman nodded. "Yes, I was chased. If I was not so swift, I would be dead already. It did not chase me beyond the town limits for which I am most grateful."

She was lying, Chaville was certain. Florian and the reports from the scouts made no mention of a demon resembling the Gate Guardian from Ouvergarde Castle being present in Autun. The castle demons were from Za and the Autun invaders were from Kee. And the scent of pine? He should have realised straight away what that meant. She was a Blood Moon. Was Chaville too close to their territory or was he a target?

Chaville helped the woman to her feet, spotting the pack that she wore on her back. Whatever was inside would no doubt be used to kill him. "Can you lead me to the entrance to Autun?" asked Chaville.

The woman nodded and turned towards the town. Chaville pounced and wrapped his arm around her neck, pulling tightly. She struggled, desperately trying to fight against the formidable paladin. She was far stronger than she looked, but could not overpower him. Moments later, she lost consciousness and fell limp in his arms.

Chaville checked the road to make sure no others were waiting in ambush, then bound her hands. He threw her over Avalanche and made for the edge of the forest where they would not be disturbed.

The paladin checked his surroundings, still not convinced she was alone, and then tied her to a tree. He took her pack and began to search through it.

"What do we have here?" he muttered to himself, pulling out a mask of gold. It was patterned like a monarch butterfly, but this woman was neither a butterfly nor a queen. She was a vicious snake.

He searched each nook and cranny of the pack, finding daggers, vials of poison, scraps of wrapped food and, most curiously, a ring with a crystal that glowed faintly and swirled with white. There was no mistaking it, this woman was a Blood Moon assassin.

Chaville sat and waited for the woman to wake, letting Avalanche graze. The assassin was quite beautiful, her sharp features less common in Roch than in other territories. A shame she chose a life that only sought to deprive others of theirs.

She finally began to stir. "What...where...am I?"

"Good," said Chaville. "I was wondering if you were going to sleep all the way to sundown. I contemplated leaving you here, but it would have been a tad cruel. I'm confident I heard a wolf howling minutes ago."

Joiselle struggled against her bindings, trying to slip her arm through the ropes. "Release me, you savage."

"No. You are going to stay put and you are going to answer my questions. I have no qualms about killing you, considering your nature."

"What do you mean?" asked Joiselle. Suddenly, her eyes widened. "Return my ring to me."

Chaville held up a hand, demanding she keep silent. "You are in no position to make demands. Do not forget that I am in control of your life right now. You cannot break free of these binds and you are no threat to me in this position. In your hubris, you thought you could outsmart me. Do you think me some rank amateur?"

Joiselle glared at him, but did not speak.

"Why did you attack me?" asked the paladin. "Answer me. Now!"

"You are my bounty," she replied simply.

"That does not make sense to me. Why disarm yourself and try to lead me into the city? Perhaps you were hoping that something would kill me instead?"

Joiselle closed her eyes, not wanting to confirm Chaville's theory.

"This would suggest to me that I am not *your* bounty, Joiselle. How do I know that? Your ring is white, not red. What that does mean, of course, is that I am somebody else's bounty and you killing me would mean excommunication. Oh yes, I know how it works."

"Do not claim to know the inner workings of the Order of the Blood Moon," spat Joiselle, her anger growing. "We have secrets and resources far greater than you could possibly imagine."

"You have your secrets, but the Outer Sentinels are more knowledgeable than *you* could possibly imagine. I know what the colour of your ring means. I know that the souls of your targets are contained within. You are trying to sabotage a fellow member, which leads me to my next question...who? Who are you trying to sabotage by ensuring my death first?"

"If you return my mask and ring, then I will tell you what you want to know. It is a very simple proposal and not of any consequence to you, surely?"

Chaville shook his head. "I'm afraid that I

cannot allow that. This ring is evil and prevents the natural flow of the dead to the Inner World. Your Moonlight Queen will not be receiving these souls. The ring will be taken to one of our churches to be destroyed and the souls will be set free. May they find peace in the Inner World at last, free from the clutches of your twisted little sect."

Joiselle screamed in horror. "No! Please, anything but that. I beg of you, Outer Sentinel. Show mercy on me."

"Your protests will do you no good. If the punishment from the Blood Moons for your betrayal of another member is death, then that is of no consequence to me. Your fate is your own doing. You ask for mercy, yet you show zero remorse for your cruelty."

Joiselle yelled and spat, cursing Chaville's name; all forms of pleading discarded. He hurled her weapons over the trees and far into the forest where they would not be easy to find. He dumped her pack onto the ground and smashed the poison vials, just to disarm her that little bit further should she escape and decide to pursue him.

He left the rest of the assassin's possessions in the dirt, taking both the ring and mask with him. These were far too precious to toss into the wild, no, they would need to be destroyed by divine magic.

The paladin climbed atop his horse once more and trotted back to the main path, Joiselle's cries and screams following him. He wished he did not, but he felt somewhat sorrowful. He pitied the woman, wondering what had led her down this path, but he was also glad that she attempted to attack him.

He did not know what drew the watchful eye of the deceased queen's evil magic to him, but he was certain that she was going to watch him live a long life until his soul departed peacefully for the Inner World where he would dwell in the True One's domain for all eternity.

Chapter 7

A Ruined Town

The Fat Demon was nowhere to be seen, but his stomps could be heard echoing in the distance. He was slow and powerful, but Tarn was fast and nimble. If he kept out of sight, the demon should not be a problem.

The assassin slid down the edge of the building, careful to land softly. Who knows what other demons were waiting nearby? He walked through the streets, cloaked in the shadow of the mountain. It would be midday before Autun saw true light, which was all the better for Tarn.

He slinked along, keeping one eye in front and the other scanning the side streets. He spied the occasional dark, hunched figure, but he did not focus on them. He needed to get the lay of the land before finding somewhere to hide until Chaville arrived. Once he knew the area, he would watch the demons and learn how they acted.

Tarn rounded a corner and spotted a stone bridge a hundred feet overhead. It was an odd sight in such a small town, perhaps the town continued into the mountainside. There must be a way to reach it.

"Gragh!" yelled a voice.

The assassin dodged, narrowly avoiding a spear piercing his side. A loosely armoured demon drew back his spear, ready to strike again. Tarn turned to the side, grabbed the spear and pulled the demon forward. It lost its balance, falling face-first into Tarn's sword with a bloody squelch.

He withdrew his sword and tossed the demon aside. He spied another demon, with its spear at the ready, approaching him. He ran towards the demon and leapt over its spear, impaling it with his dagger.

The demon fell backwards and Tarn climbed off. He could hear the stomping of the Fat Demon growing closer, being drawn in by the commotion. Tarn jumped on a nearby crate, using it to grab onto an awning. He pulled himself up and ran up the wall, vaulting himself over the edge and onto the roof.

The Fat Demon rounded the corner and immediately spotted the two dead demons. He ran up to each and picked it up with his stubby fingers. He looked at them closely, before sniffing them. With shocking force, he threw them across the town, where they landed streets away. Tarn was more assured than ever that he should avoid this behemoth.

The assassin waited for it to resume its patrol, then stood up. The best thing he could do right now was to avoid the streets. He hopped over to the next roof. It was slippery, but Tarn was just dextrous enough to keep his footing.

He leapt across a few more roofs, taking in each street and every alleyway. He was sure that he could deal with Chaville in a single strike if he had the element of surprise. If he wasn't able to catch him unawares, he needed every advantage he could get.

"Hmm," said the assassin, pondering what to do. There were no more roofs he could reach without breaking his neck. He would have to take to the streets for a while. He dropped to a window ledge, then onto the brickwork path. The stomps of the Fat Demon were but a muffled thud. It was safe enough here, at least for now.

Tarn ran across a walkway that ran over a slow-moving canal. For all his skills, Tarn was not a strong swimmer and would avoid this area where possible. At the far side of the walkway, there was a cluster of makeshift wooden barricades. They had rusty nails hammered into them, perhaps an attempt by the former townsfolk to prevent the demons from crossing into this side of town.

The assassin hurdled over one and ascended a small staircase. He could see two more demons ahead, one wielding a crude sword and the other gripping both a spear and a shield. They had yet to notice him, so he slipped behind the corner of a building.

He climbed through a window and moved across the room to reach the doorway. He opened it slowly, careful not to let it creak. The demons were standing still, looking in the opposite direction.

Tarn crept towards them with his dagger drawn. He quickly despatched the nearest one, the one with the sword. As it fell to the floor with a clunk, Tarn hurled his dagger at the demon with the shield and spear, but it was too quick. It turned and the dagger narrowly missed, landing halfway down the street ahead.

The demon snarled and raised its shield, charging at Tarn with its spear poking out from a hole near the top of the shield. Tarn waited for it to strike and grabbed the spear, but the demon bashed him with the shield, knocking the assassin back.

"Come and get me," uttered Tarn as he allowed the demon to back him into a corner. When the demon drew close, the assassin stepped onto the wall and leapt over the demon, drawing his sword down in an arc. He dragged the blade across the demon's scalp, cutting his ugly head vertically in two.

When the demon had fallen to the floor, a slow clapping began. A man with a shaved head and a rat-like face was sitting on a wall nearby. He was wearing leather armour, but it was much uglier than Tarn's. He had his own short sword and dagger hanging from his belt and a crossbow strapped to his back.

"That was quite the manoeuvre, mate," he said enthusiastically. "Where'd a fella like you learn how to do that?"

Tarn stared at him, without answering.

"Come now, I ain't here to cause trouble. I'm a simple treasure hunter looking to relieve the dead and the damned of their worldly possessions. No use for those in the Inner World or the hells. I suppose you could even call them their former possessions, eh?"

Tarn walked down the street and retrieved his dagger, not taking his eyes off the man. "What do you want?" he asked at last.

"Me? I don't want nothing," said the man with a chuckle. "I just happened upon your little scuffle and thought I would observe. There's not a lot of action here outside of the fat bloke wandering past every now and then. He's best avoided, he is."

"Who are you?" asked Tarn, eyeing the man suspiciously.

"Ah, it's an introduction you would like then? I'm happy to oblige, my masked friend. Name's Alvaro. I'm a simple treasure hunter, like I said earlier."

"You call yourself a treasure hunter, but you described a looter."

"Marketing, my friend. If I call myself a looter, it don't sound like a great introduction. Call me a looter if you want, but I'm sticking with treasure hunter." Alvaro tapped on his forehead. "You're probably not one to talk, being an assassin and all."

"You can think what you want of me and my profession, I do not care. I will serve the Moonlight Queen until my dying day, and continue to pray that that day comes after she returns to this world."

"Ah, you're not a regular, old assassin then. You're one of the Blood Moons. I probably should have worked it out, seeing that red ring of yours. A fancy trinket, no doubt. I guess there's no point in me trying to hire you then, is there?"

"My skills are not for sale. At the very least, not while I'm on a mission."

"Who are you looking for? Perhaps ol' Alvaro can help?"

"No," said Tarn, his distaste for the thief growing by the second.

"Come on now, lad. If I wanted to attack you, I would have blasted a hole through you with this gal during your little brawl," said Alvaro, patting his crossbow. "I'm one of the best shots you'll ever see, so don't think I couldn't. You've got to trust somebody every now and then."

Tarn could see that Alvaro was the sort of man that you could immediately tell did not have a moral bone in his body. He had no code nor ethics and that made him a man purely driven by incentives. Tarn would have to appeal to that malleability.

He relented at last. At the very least, he could be kept out of the way if he could not be of assistance. "I'm seeking an Outer Sentinel called Chaville. I do not know what he looks like, other than he tends to wear a helmet. I have it on good authority that he was making his way to this town."

Alvaro's eyes lit up with glee and he howled with laughter. "You're going to bury an Outer Sentinel? I would pay a good few silvers to see that."

"Have you seen him or not?"

"I'm afraid I ain't seen him," said Alvaro, looking towards an approaching armoured demon, drawn in by his raucous laughter. "I got this one, mate."

The thief loaded up his crossbow and fired at the demon, landing a shot square between its eyes. Alvaro was not lying about his accuracy. The demon was near a hundred feet away and Alvaro had barely taken the time to aim.

"You have not seen him?" asked Tarn.

"Nope, but I can tell you where he's probably heading. An Outer Sentinel would be looking for the biggest demon scores he could get, wouldn't you say? First, he would be aiming for fatty across the canal, but that hefty chap is a minor win compared to what's waiting some ways up the mountain."

"What would that be?"

Alvaro smiled deviously. "A Temple of the True One that's been taken by the demons. They've turned it into a Temple of Mallabeth. You wonder why there ain't that many dead bodies around here, mostly skeletons, right? You'd think the place would be littered with corpses, particularly considering a few folk are stupid enough to wander in here every day."

"Go on," ordered Tarn, listening intently.

"Well, what I reckon they're doing up there is some sort of sacrifice. Mallabeth, the Inner World god of the undead and all that, is going to want all that blood and flesh. The bones may be useful, but bones are plentiful and don't decay. The flesh needs to be grabbed good and quick. If I were an Outer Sentinel, that would be my target...but I ain't one, so I hang about here hunting for treasure."

Alvaro flexed and wriggled his ten digits, as though he was a gluttonous oaf looking at the last slice of pie. As much as Tarn disliked him, he was a good source of information. He still wasn't convinced that he wouldn't be shot in the back as he walked away, so he needed some assurance that he would be permitted to leave unscathed. Tarn reached into his pack and flipped a silver coin towards the man.

"You're as cunning as you are a good shot," said Tarn. "If you're right about this, I will see to it that you're handsomely rewarded. I don't have a lot of coin on me, I travel light, but I will see that you get some gold for your troubles. The Moonlight Queen provides and my order is well cared for, as are those who aid us."

"Mighty generous of you, mate," said Alvaro eyeing up the immaculate ounce of silver. "What would it be worth to you if Chaville comes this way and I make sure he gets tired out before reaching the temple? It would make your job a lot easier, just saying."

"Two and a half ounces of gold. Make sure the Fat Demon and the rest of these weaklings do not kill him. He's no good to me already dead, that's not how our bounties work."

"Two and a half ounces you say?"

"Yes," said Tarn with a nod. "I don't need gold, I need something much more valuable."

Alvaro hopped off the wall and walked over to Tarn, reaching out his hand. Tarn shook it, with no intent on ever making good on this promise. Once he collected Chaville's soul for his Queen, he would avoid the sneaky thief like the plague.

"How do I reach the bridge overhead?" asked the assassin.

"There's a tower built into the side of the mountain, about half a mile away," said Alvaro pointing over the wall he had been sitting on. "You'll be able to see it once you round the corner."

"Wait at the bridge for me once Chaville has made his way to the temple," said Tarn. "We will deal with your reward once my business with him is complete. Thank you, Alvaro."

"A pleasure, friend," said Alvaro with a sickening grin.

Tarn jumped over the small wall and dashed off. He did not look over his shoulder, but he could feel Alvaro's eyes on the back of his head. If Chaville was sent to the temple, exhausted and ready to fall, then Alvaro will have served his purpose. What happened next to the sharpshooting thief was of no concern to Tarn.

The assassin climbed a staircase and rounded a corner. He weaved through the streets, stealthily killing the occasional demon, wanting to be out of the thief's line of sight.

True to what Alvaro had said, the tower came into view. It was indeed built into the mountainside, bearing small windows on the way up that would have been used to survey most of the town.

Tarn walked inside and could see the staircase on his left spiralling upwards towards the ceiling. His eyes followed it upwards, and it brought him back to his escape from the keep. He brought his eyes back down and began his ascension.

Each time he reached a window, the assassin glanced out at the town stretching out before him. He absorbed new details with each survey. Should the worst come to pass, he would at least be familiar enough with the town to find a new way to use the terrain against Chaville.

At the top of the tower, there was a stone archway with a wooden door. Was that music coming from the other side? Tarn listened closely and could hear the faint sound of a flute.

He cautiously opened the door and looked outside. The stone bridge stretched across the valley towards the other side of the mountain. Sat on the low wall of the bridge was an old man in yellow robes, playing his flute.

Chapter 8

Trimming the Fat

Chaville walked up the road towards Autun, alone. He had found a quiet place to tie up Avalanche, where he would be safe from demons until his master returned.

The town was in bad shape, that was clear even from this distance. The demons had not been kind, particularly the Fat Demon. The walls of buildings were torn down and roofs were broken, missing half of their slates that lay as shattered fragments of clay on the streets.

As Chaville approached, the remnants of the chaotic fall of Autun became more apparent. Where the skeletal and rotted remains of the citizens lay, he knelt and said a prayer. These people, whatever their sins, did not deserve this fate.

The town was quiet at the moment, but the paladin did not expect that to last. He could smell the demons from here, the smell of ash and sulphur was unmistakable. Even having grown so accustomed to this smell, Chaville was sickened by it.

He paused, a short way down the street and listened. The sound of faint stomps in the distance reached his ears, but there was something closer. It was the sound of armour clinking.

Chaville drew his claymore and closed his eyes, listening for the direction of his stalker. Was this the assassin? No, too heavy-footed. It was a demon lurking nearby, perhaps drawn in by the paladin's own noisy armour.

A low hiss broke from the demon as it thrust a spear towards the man. He swept the attack away and barged the demon to the ground. He skewered it in the gut and sought cover in an alley.

The sound of the stomping footsteps drew closer and Chaville waited. There was no sense in letting it spot him first. No, the element of surprise was certainly his friend here.

The paladin leaned around the corner, trying to catch a glimpse of his target. There it was, towering over a small building a few streets away. It was indeed fat, and it was most certainly ugly. Its smile was as grotesque as the acidic boils that covered its stretched flesh. As it rounded a corner, its bone club came into view. Being hit by the full weight of that would be certain death, armour or no armour.

Chaville stepped back into the shadows and cast the Holy Steel spell, readying himself for the bloated behemoth that was steadily approaching his position.

The stomping grew louder and louder. The paladin waited for the monster to pass, then ran out, slashing at its heels. The Fat Demon let out a warbling roar of pain, the stench of its putrid breath permeated the air. Men with weaker stomachs would have been brought to their knees.

The demon wildly stomped and swung its club. It had no rhyme or reason, it just wanted to cause as much damage as it could to whoever had attacked it.

Chaville stood back, making sure no other demons were closing in on him. The Fat Demon began to calm down, the effects of the divine energy enchanting Chaville's blade not enough to kill it. It spotted the paladin in the street and its ugly snarl turned into a lecherous grin.

It reached forward a hand, trying to grab the man, intending to make him a part of its next meal. With no desire to be eaten, Chaville thrust his claymore into its palm.

The stupid brute recoiled again and ripped its hand away, pulling Chaville's sword with it. The paladin was weaponless, but he was not deterred. He had fought foes like this unarmed before and was still here to tell the tale.

As the Fat Demon swung its club at him, he used his Push spell to redirect the blow. The bone club collided with a nearby building, smashing its front wall to pieces and sending a cascade of rubble across the street. Chaville ducked to avoid the larger pieces and his armour shielded him from the smaller fragments.

The paladin grabbed onto the demon's heel,

right where he had wounded it and cast his True Touch spell. He sent a wave of divine energy throughout the infernal beast's body. He willed more and more energy into the wound, and the demon yelled, vibrating vigorously.

It slammed its elbow upon the top of Chaville's helmet, knocking the paladin to the moss-covered bricks. He was dazed, but lucid enough to roll over as the demon's club came flying through the air. It dozens of bricks, leaving the street in an even worse state than before.

Chaville stood up and grabbed a large, jagged stone that had broken off the nearby wall. He reached back and hurled the stone at one of the demon's boils, which burst and sent viscous pus splashing onto the street. The Fat Demon howled furiously before shaking himself off, but Chaville was already upon him.

The paladin took hold of the demon's leg once again, where the burn of his True Touch was still raw. He sent the divine spell flowing from his hands and through the Fat Demon once again, but this time he gripped tighter than ever.

The beast tried to pull its leg away, but Chaville was unrelenting. He dug his fingers into the demon, piercing its skin and holding onto its flesh from within. Its boils began to burst and sent acidic pus raining from the sky. It burned Chaville's skin where it breached the gaps in his armour, but he continued to hold on.

The demon suddenly went limp and fell to the ground, landing with a crash on the street and shattering many cobblestones. It was dead. No longer a threat to any poor soul who should pass through Autun.

The paladin pulled his sword from the beast's hand and sought refuge in a nearby building. He removed parts of his armour and tended to his burns. It was painful to heal, but he gritted his teeth and cast his spell. The intensity of his spellcasting took a lot out of him, but he only allowed himself to rest momentarily. Once he was confident that he would have no lingering effects from the Fat Demon's pus, he returned to the street in search of the route to the bridge.

As Chaville walked through the town, he cut down more demons. They were few and far between, possibly the result of a valiant last stand by the citizens. Perhaps there were far more awaiting him at the desecrated temple?

Chaville squinted, spotting the silhouette of a man in the distance. Was it another demon? No, it was no demon; it was indeed a man.

He was sitting casually on a low rooftop, as though the town was in no trouble whatsoever. He smiled an unconvincing smile and waved Chaville forward. The paladin would have to stay on his guard, perhaps this was the Blood Moon assassin that was hunting him? Surely he would not be so brazen.

The man hopped down from the roof with ease and approached Chaville, his hands raised to show he was not holding a weapon. He was not wearing a ring, perhaps this man was not the assassin after all? Granted, neither was Joiselle, so he should remain vigilant. The paladin slung his sword over his back, ready to use magic should he need to.

"Good day," said Chaville.

"Same to you, mate," said Alvaro jovially. "I hope it will be all the better for our meeting. Hard to find folks who don't want to kill you in a town like this, eh?"

"Indeed. What is your name, stranger?" asked Chaville.

"Me? I'm Chatou," said the man. He had a rat-like face that only a mother could love, but even she would struggle.

"Chatou? The bard?" asked Chaville, unconvinced. The man was very chipper for a fellow who had both lost his people and his home to demons.

"Yip, that would be me, mate," said Alvaro, trying hard to avoid his usual sneer, but he played it as cool as he could muster.

"You don't look much like a bard."

"Of course not," said Alvaro, producing a broken flute. "You think I prance around in a funny getup playing the flute when there are demons in my town? You must be having a laugh. I'm packed and ready to punch through a few infernal skulls. Ain't nothing else for it in times like this. Believe you me, I would love nothing else than to be sitting in a tavern, drunk and merry, singing my songs."

Perhaps Chaville had misjudged the man? "I meant no disrespect. My name is Chaville. I'm one of the Outer Sentinels. You sent word to my sect and they've sent me to help cleanse this town on behalf of the True One. I've already dealt with the big lad. Are there any other demons of note around here before I start sorting out the mere minions?"

"Outer Sentinel, eh? I've been waiting on you a while, mate. The town's gone to hell and back, all thanks to them fellas across the bridge up there." Alvaro pointed to the bridge that stretched above the valley.

"Dare I ask what awaits me up there?"

"I don't know, if I'm honest with you, mate. I've only been as far as the bridge itself. I've seen 'em carrying the dead up there for who knows what. Wouldn't go up there even if you paid me an ounce of gold. Maybe for ten ounces, but even then it would just be to take a quick peek and scurry back down again."

"Fear not, good bard. I do not need to know what is up there, but it would of course help. I shall see to it that whatever demons plague the temple are brought to a swift end, then the refugees can return and finally start to rebuild. I fear no evil, and neither should you."

"Awfully good of you, sir paladin. I'll show you the way up and make sure you get there all safe. In fact, I'll come with you to the top and wait at the bridge. Don't have the nerve in me to help you in the temple, I'm afraid, but I'll be cheering you on."

"I would appreciate that, Chatou," said Chaville. He did not like the look of this man one bit, but he was going to give him the benefit of the doubt. A single toe out of line and he would find himself at the bottom of the canal with zero remorse spared by the paladin.

Alvaro led Chaville through the streets, careful to check around each corner for lingering demons.

"That big thud I heard earlier," said Alvaro. "Was that what I think it was? The big lad, you called him?"

"Yes," replied Chaville proudly, "the Fat Demon is no more. Its death is the first step in me giving this town back to you and your people. There will be more evil blood spilled before the end, but I assure you that it will be done. I have dealt with demons like this for most of my life and I am still here to tell the tale."

"Cor," marvelled Alvaro, genuinely impressed by Chaville. "I wouldn't want to get on your bad side, I'll tell you that. I've done my best to avoid the Fat Demon like the plague. Mind you, he looked like he was suffering from the plague. Those awful boils could melt a hole in the stone. Easy."

Chaville stopped waking, no longer listening to the man. He spotted a mess of red and yellow along a side street, not far from the river. Something was amiss.

"Hold on," he said, walking over to inspect.

Alvaro followed as Chaville knelt down and examined the gruesome scene before them. It was a man wearing yellow robes, covered in his own blood. He looked barely human, his body contorted in awkward angles. He had taken a hard hit and that was putting it very mildly indeed.

"What happened here then?" asked Alvaro, placing his hand on the broken flute and gripping it tightly. "Big fatty get to him just before you got here or what?"

"No," said Chaville, looking upon the dead and broken man. "He fell."

"Fell from where?"

Chaville pointed upwards to the bridge. "He fell from there, and it must have been within the last few hours. There's something on the bridge, perhaps waiting for us, perhaps making its way to the desecrated temple," Chaville shook his head wearily. "I do not feel good about this in the least. We should be very careful, Chatou. Even if you have been fine here for some time, we must remain extra vigilant."

"That we should, mate. It's like I said, I dare not cross that thing unless I can help it. Probably demons sitting there waiting for hapless fools like us. If we toddle on up, they'll toss us off the edge like a child throwing stones into a pond. What do you reckon?"

"It's definitely possible," muttered the paladin. He was not convinced. He knew that the pair were not alone in Autun. There were demons aplenty, yes, but the Blood Moon assassin was nowhere to be seen. Had this been the case of a mistaken target? Was Chaville the one who should have been pushed from the bridge?

"Let's get out of here," said Alvaro, eager to leave the scene. "Always best not to stay in one place too long, that's my motto. If there's a dead body, I'm sure the demons will be here before long. They always take them to the Temple of Mallabeth up top."

Chaville nodded slowly. "Yes, I suspect it will do us no good lingering here."

The paladin felt more uneasy than he had felt in some time. He followed Alvaro down the street towards a large tower built into the side of the mountain. It reached all the way to the bridge, and would carry him further along the path to his destination.

Chapter 9

The Temple of Flesh

Tarn stood by and watched as the old man played his flute. The song was slow and pleasant, a serenade to the town below. A town that could not hear his song. Tarn approached quietly and stood behind the man, who continued to play until his song was over. The last note hung in the air, carried by the slight breeze that blew across the bridge.

"Greetings," said the man solemnly.

"What are you doing?" asked Tarn curiously.

"I am playing music. I can think of nothing better to do right now," sighed the man. "You are more than welcome to stay and listen."

"Why are you playing? You must know the state of things below. This place is dangerous for far more formidable men than you."

"It is because of the state of things that I play. My town is filled with hostile invaders who both slaughtered my people and turned some of them into their own. When there is such darkness, surely there must be some merriment brought back to a place like this, no?"

"Merriment?"

"I don't know what else you would call it, my friend. Happiness? Ease? There must be something to lift the spirits of the dead as they make their way to the Inner World. I have prayed until I can pray no more, so perhaps this will also help? If my song can nudge their souls an inch in the right direction, I've done something good in this forsaken hellhole."

"I do not understand," said Tarn, convinced the man had gone crazy from grief.

"You do not need to understand. Please sit and listen for a while. I believe it will ease your troubled soul."

"I have somewhere I need to be."

"You have come all this way to Autun, so take a few minutes to rest," insisted the man. "There is nowhere you need to be so badly that you can not spare a few minutes."

"Alright," said Tarn, finally caving into the man's request.

He stood back from the wall, not wanting to risk being thrown from the edge by a devious trick, but he let the man play his song. The peaceful melody called out in the morning air, seeking ears to fill with its splendour. It was not loud enough to carry to the town below, but the man did not care. He played and he played. The assassin forgot time and stood there for a half hour as the music man took him on a journey of highs and lows.

Tarn closed his eyes and imagined a sprawling field filled with knee-high green grass. Deep green, not the brownish-yellow of the grass in these cold parts. The mountains were far in the distance and stretched far higher than any man would dare climb. There was no need to hunt anymore, for the Moonlight Queen was already here. She had given her followers bliss and let them wander the land freely without a care, without a burden.

As the song faded, the man turned towards Tarn. "Do you feel better?" he asked with genuine curiosity.

Tarn laughed quietly. "I believe so. It was a pleasant song. What do you call it?"

"It does not have a name, I made it up as I played. I suspect I will not remember it as I haven't written down the notes. It is a one-of-a-kind treat for both you and me. A unique experience that bonds us together in a memory that will die along with us. It's something special, isn't it?"

"You're a strange fellow."

"So I have been told many times," chuckled the man, seeming momentarily happy, "but I play a mean flute. The people here used to tell me that often too."

"What's your name, old man?"

"My name is Chatou. What about you, Blood Moon?"

"You know of the Order? My name is Tarn."

"I am aware of only a little. I did not know that your kind hunted demons...unless you are here for me? I should hope not because I suspect I won't stand a chance. I survive here only because I'm good at keeping to myself."

"You are safe," Tarn assured him. "I am paying a visit to the Temple of the True One."

"It is a temple to Mallabeth now, I'm sad to inform you. The minions of a fallen angel have taken up residence in a sacred holy place. It is debased and corrupted. I suggest you go elsewhere if that is at all possible."

"I don't have a choice in the matter," lamented Tarn.

"Ah, a target is there? I should have realised sooner. I don't believe there is anybody left alive in that accursed temple. The only one below is the ugly man with the crossbow. I would avoid him too now that I think about it. Perhaps you are going to wait for somebody in the temple?"

"Perhaps I am. Can I trust that you will keep my presence a secret? It is of the utmost importance to me. It can serve to strengthen our bond further, another unique moment that compliments your song."

Chatou laughed again, his spirits lifted slightly. It did not matter to him that the man he was speaking to was a deadly assassin, for he had enjoyed the song. "I am not much of a talker these days; I prefer to play my music. I'm awaiting the Outer Sentinels arriving to cleanse the town. I sent word some time ago, but they are stretched thin these days. Troubled times we live in. It goes far beyond Autun."

The man started to play once more, believing Tarn was assured he would remain tight-lipped. The assassin's heart was heavy. It was this man who had called upon Chaville to vanquish the demons in the town. He could not risk Chaville knowing of his presence, even if the man did not have any ill intent towards him. The mere mention of Blood Moon could ring alarm bells to the Sentinel.

Tarn closed his eyes momentarily, taking in the song. There was nothing else he could do. He slowly edged his way to the wall. He raised his hands, but they were shaking. A sacrifice in the name of the Moonlight Queen is acceptable, nay, it is necessary. A murder of an innocent old man...surely not?

Tarn hesitated. No, he could not do it. This man was playing a song while awaiting a saviour for his town. He did not deserve death for merely being in the wrong place at the wrong time. However, service to the Moonlight Queen comes before all.

The assassin held his breath and shoved Chatou as he played his song on the wall. Tarn tried to block out the scream as the man fell to his death on the stone below.

"I am sorry," muttered Tarn, as he looked over the edge. The man lay broken on the ground, barely distinguishable from this distance.

The assassin had no choice, that's what he told himself. The risk was too great and the bounty must be claimed. To not claim a bounty was to be excommunicated and he could not allow that to happen. The Moonlight Queen must be revived and brought back to the Outer World.

The assassin stood at the edge of the bridge and stared across the town. He watched until the sun was overhead, illuminating the abandoned settlement. It was a beautiful place. It was a shame what had happened here, but not of great surprise.

Tarn decided to stop wallowing and crossed the

bridge. It was laden with rubble and broken barricades, ending in a large archway which led to a rough path up the mountain. Pine trees lined each side of the path and sporadic stone steps were placed along it to guide the way.

The assassin stayed to the left of the path, careful not to run afoul of any demons. If Alvaro was correct, it wouldn't be long before Chatou's body was carried up here to be sacrificed to Mallabeth.

Tarn watched the path as he ascended. It started to morph from a slope with the occasional step into more intricate brickwork, then finally into a fully paved pathway. It was not long before he reached a wall that led into a courtyard.

Tarn climbed one of the pine trees and leapt onto the wall, gripping the edge. He pulled himself up just enough to see the courtyard. It was a mess of debris and bones, with demons loitering throughout the compound. The bricks on both the walls and the ground were stained with blood, with the ones on the wall looking like drag marks. A brutal slaughter had taken place here.

The assassin crept along sideways, keeping a tight grip on the edge of the wall. Once he reached a small watchtower at the corner, he pulled himself up and dove into the tower. He could see the temple clearly from here, sitting at the far end of the courtyard atop a flight of stairs.

It was a grand building with intricately carved statues and sculptures across the front wall, with large wooden doors that were sealed tightly. At the furthest side, a tower erupted from the roof, leading to a belfry where a large bronze bell hung. Unlike Chatou's flute, the toll of the bell would easily carry to the people of Autun.

As much as he would have loved to wait for nightfall, the assassin could not afford to do so. He climbed out of the tower and lowered himself onto the wall once more. He quickly moved each hand, shimmying himself along. Every so often, he would peer over and into the courtyard to check his location.

When he had reached close enough to the steps into the temple, Tarn threw himself over the wall and sought refuge behind a ransacked wagon. Whatever goods it had brought to the temple were long gone and the wagon was missing a wheel.

Tarn peered out from behind the wagon to check if the coast was clear, but it was not. An armoured demon, more heavily armoured than those in town, stood guarding the door. It had a single eye and a gaping socket where the second eye should be. Its horns were two long curves, not unlike the horns of a ram, while its hands ended in large claws that did not match the rest of its body.

Perhaps it was stupid? Tarn grabbed a piece of loose wood from the wagon and hurled it at the demon. As soon as the wood was within a few feet of the clawed guard, it smashed it into splinters with its left claw. It turned towards the wagon and walked to the base of the steps.

Tarn kept low, leaning against the wagon, waiting for it to approach. He was ready to strike the moment it came into view. Tarn suddenly fell backwards as the wagon was thrown into the air by the clawed demon. It yelled in its demonic tongue and lunged at the assassin, who rolled backwards and just out of reach.

Reluctant to attract more attention, Tarn ran

back up the wall and grabbed the ledge. To his surprise, the clawed demon swiped at the wall, bringing it down and sending Tarn down with it. Tarn rolled down the mountainside and collided with one of the pine trees.

The demon charged at him with its claws raised. Tarn scurried up the tree as the demon lunged. The tree was felled and Tarn jumped off and stabbed the demon in the neck with his short sword. It roared in pain, trying to pull the blade from the gap in its armour.

Tarn grabbed the handle and placed a foot on its chest, pulling the blade free and setting the clawed demon off balance on the slope. He gave it a heavy kick with his boot and it fell forwards, tumbling down the mountainside.

The assassin quickly scrambled up the rocky slope and through the large gap in the wall. He checked for any demons approaching to investigate the loud commotion, but they had left the clawed demon to deal with it. Perhaps it was feared even amongst the other demons?

Tarn ran up the staircase and grabbed onto a pillar by the door. He furiously pulled himself up, praying the demons would not notice him. As he climbed, a fireball whizzed past his hood, hitting the carvings on the temple wall.

He glanced over his shoulder and spied the demon soldiers charging towards him. Each raised a hand to hurl a Fireball spell at him. He did not want to meet the same fate that he granted the Tree Mother.

Tarn leapt from the pillar to the wall of the temple, clinging to a small cherub's arm. He zigzagged his way upwards, the edges of his hood and armour taking a few singes.

As Tarn reached for the roof, one of the spells caught him on the arm. He grimaced, but pulled himself up and over. He did not let himself yell, in fear of attracting more attention.

He ran across the roof and reached for the ladder on the wall of the bell tower. If it was not safe in here, at least he could kick his enemies from a great height and send them to their much-deserved deaths.

Each movement of Tarn's left arm was agonising, the burn starting to take effect. He pushed ahead and threw himself on the floor of the tower.

The large bronze bell loomed over him, old and a greyish-green colour. Tarn sat up and looked to the roof below. There was another ladder visible in a small alcove, presumably leading to the upper floor of the temple. He waited, expecting a visit from the demonic soldiers, but they never arrived.

"Most odd," said Tarn. He waited until the sun began to set, but he heard no commotion. He could still see demons in the courtyard, but no sign of Chaville.

The assassin thought that he might as well investigate rather than twiddle his thumbs atop the lonely tower. As beautiful as the sunset stretching over the pine forest was, he had no desire to sit there all night. He slid down the ladder, as darkness encroached, and the moon appeared in the sky from behind the clouds.

He trod softly along the slate tiles, careful not to alert the demons in case they had a change of heart about pursuing him on the roof. He reached the ladder and lowered himself down.

Tarn descended into a small chamber, lit by faint torchlight from the large hall below. He walked over to a wooden barrier and looked down.

The room was tall and long, not unusual for the various worshipping houses of the True One spread throughout the Outer World. It was lined with statues of angels, all of which had their stone wings clipped and their heads forcibly removed. Each was stained with blood, marking the temple in the name of Mallabeth.

The statues weren't what caught Tarn's eye the most. His eyes wandered past the pews towards the far end of the room. In front of the grandest desecrated statue stood a man. However, it was not an ordinary man.

This man was tall, twice the size of Tarn. He was bulky, muscular and deformed. He wore a mask made of skull fragments that were not atop his face. No, they were embedded into it. Random bones and bulbous protrusions broke through his skin, making him seem even more imposing.

"A flesh golem?" Tarn muttered. He was now more certain than ever that Alvaro was right. An Outer Sentinel could not leave a place like this alone.

Flesh golems were rare among the golem constructs, but the most reviled. Where a flesh golem resided, evil sat along with it. Evil divine magic and infernal sorcery combined into one being; the power of necromancy. A greater abomination could not be found across the Outer World.

Tarn had to get a better view. He slowly climbed over the barrier and onto the wooden beams supporting the ceiling. He moved to the right side of the room and waited by a pillar, ensuring he had a good view of both the golem and the door.

He would watch the mutilated, stitched-together remains of the townsfolk until the Outer Sentinel arrived to slay it. Then he would make his move.

Chapter 10

The Worm's Deception

Alvaro led Chaville up the tower, making small talk about various nonsense topics as he did so. The paladin wasn't sure if the supposed bard was trying to be friendly or if he was trying to distract himself from whatever may await them on the bridge. Whatever the reason, it was irritating him greatly.

As they reached the top of the tower, Alvaro turned to Chaville. "This is where I leave you, mate."

The paladin nodded. "I appreciate your help, Chatou. Good luck with whatever it is you're still doing here. I don't believe I ever asked?"

"Seeking inspiration, my friend. It's one thing

to write songs about things from your imagination, it's another to write from lived experience. The audience appreciates it. Got to keep 'em enchanted by the tales, right?"

"I suppose so," said Chaville, not convinced by the answer.

"Can't forget that this place is my home. I think I'd like to stick around and see if you can bring it back from the brink. What a sight that would be, eh?"

"I assure you I will get it done," said Chaville. "I have dedicated my life to the True One and to the efforts of ridding the Outer World of demons."

"A noble cause. Not sure if I've got it in me, but I respect you for it."

"Thank you, Chatou," said Chaville. He gave Alvaro a salute and bid him farewell.

"Good luck, mate. You're probably gonna need it."

Alvaro started walking down the staircase as Chaville walked out onto the bridge. It was clear except for the remains of smashed barricades and bloody drag marks, not yet washed away by the rain. The sun had almost set as long shadows were cast over the town below.

Chaville looked back inside the tower, checking to see if the man he was not entirely convinced was Chatou was still walking away. Much to his relief, the man was still descending the spiral staircase.

The paladin walked across the bridge, stopping in the middle. The sun began to set as he stared across the remains of the town. It was a sad sight, even though he did not know Autun in its prime.

The Outer Sentinels feared that the end of the Dusk Era was drawing close. The unprecedented number of demon invasions was said to be what pre-dated each other apocalyptic event that brought about the end of previous eras.

The surviving texts from the end of the Dawn Era, four and a half millennia ago, told of an Outer World god's soul becoming a demonic soul. This rare event weakened the barriers between the Outer World and the hell realms. Only when the newly created demon god was slain, did the Era end for good.

Chaville shook his head. "Surely not. We could not be so close..."

He resumed his walk across the bridge. As Chaville was almost at the end, he hesitated. He contemplated turning back, but his brief thought was interrupted by a bolt piercing his shoulder.

"Agh!" yelled the paladin, diving behind a broken barricade.

"Sorry about this, mate," yelled a voice from halfway across the bridge.

"Chatou? You're the Blood Moon assassin, aren't you?" asked the paladin. He peered over the barricade and could see the rat-faced man aiming his crossbow at him.

"Me? Nah, not a Blood Moon. Just a regular old treasure hunter is the way I see it. Here for a spot of plundering."

"You're not the real Chatou, are you?"

"You ought to be a bit less trusting, friend. It made it that much easier for me. Name's Alvaro."

"The man in the yellow robes?"

"That was probably him," said Alvaro. "I found him in a heap, having fallen from this here bridge. He was kind enough to lend me his broken flute. A lucky coincidence for me, not so much for you."

"You do not want this town saved? Why do you want me dead?" demanded Chaville, buying time to heal his injured shoulder.

"I like the town this way. Makes all the goods left behind that much easier to take," said Alvaro with a smirk. "As for you? I'm not so worried about you. I'm not going to kill you, but you're certainly not crossing the bridge again."

Chaville could see the worm of a man pouring something from a flask across the bridge. He cast the Sparks spell and lit a blazing fire. He proceeded to do it again a few feet back, then a third time. If Chaville wanted to reach him, he would have to leap through three walls of fire.

"I do not understand your goal. There are plenty of places for you to loot in this town. My being here only makes it safer for you and I would have been none the wiser had you operated quietly in the background. Explain yourself."

"The inner workings of my plans are much too intricate for you to understand, mate. Just trust that I know what I'm doing."

"You're a fool," said Chaville. "A very dangerous fool. You are going to meet an unfortunate end one day, whether by my hand or by another."

"Off you go up to the temple, Sentinel," chortled Alvaro. "I'm sure the demons are eager to make your acquaintance."

Chaville stood up, his shoulder mended, and charged towards the fire. Another bolt pierced his shoulder near instantly. He dropped his claymore and fell to his knees.

"Oh no you don't," said Alvaro with a sneer. "You ain't getting past me. I could kill you if I wanted, but I've decided to show mercy on you. I'll even let you pick up your sword."

The paladin reached over to his blade and used it to push himself back to his feet. He turned and walked away from the flames, defeated and humiliated. He was angry at himself for not listening to his gut.

"The Blood Moon?" he called to Alvaro.

"Don't know what you're talking about," replied the worm. "Now get moving or I'll aim for the head next time. Want me to sing you off?"

Chaville did not answer.

Alvaro broke into song, singing the Ode to the Outer Sentinels. An encouraging song that was known across the land.

Chaville was disgusted by the mockery of the Outer Sentinels. If he could have reached him, he would have thrown Alvaro from the bridge. He gave in and walked in the direction of the temple. He had little choice left. He walked up the path and made for the trees at the edge.

After healing his wounds once more, he continued along the path as the moon emerged from behind the clouds. He could smell the demons up ahead. Perhaps this was not a Blood Moon ploy, but the efforts of a man in service of demons looking to take out an Outer Sentinel? Why not just kill him? Was Chaville meant to be an offering and they needed him alive for something? It was not adding up to the paladin.

The gates to the temple courtyard were missing, a foreboding welcome for those foolish enough to come here. Chaville could see the demons inside, all armoured and ready to fight at a moment's notice.

He clanked his sword against his breastplate,

trying to funnel the demons through the gateway. He had better odds if they weren't able to easily surround him.

"Come and face me, you hellspawn!" cried the Outer Sentinel, enraged by both the recent deception and the presence of the foul demons in a Temple of the True One.

One of the demons approached, eager to claim the kill. It lowered its horns and charged forward; its spear pointed at Chaville. The paladin used his Push spell on its legs as it grew near, and the demon fell face-first onto the stone path. Chaville raised his sword and stabbed it in the back of the head.

"One down," he muttered, as others began to approach. A half dozen demons charged at him, while others appeared atop the walls and began throwing fireballs at him.

Chaville brought the assault to the demons, dodging the fireballs and beheading the monsters. He charged inside the courtyard, determined to clear the demons above him. He could not dodge forever and there was no telling when the demons would run out of their Fireball spells.

The courtyard was filled with rubble and blood as the fire rained down from the sky. The paladin leapt up a staircase in a corner, taking three steps at a time. He barrelled down the walkway, cutting limbs and throats along the way.

He returned to the courtyard to face the rest of the demons as they emerged from the various buildings and shrines lining the temple. The only door remaining sealed was the church that stood atop a large staircase.

One demon sprayed acid from its mouth, but

Chaville dove underneath and gutted the beast. Another demon stomped on the ground, sending a shockwave across the stone bricks. Chaville spread his weight and remained standing, charging the demon once the rumbling subsided.

As Chaville made his way to the staircase night was falling and the full moon had emerged in the sky. A heavily armoured demon with two ram-like horns walked down the steps to greet him. It was wielding two large claw-like weapons. As it grew closer, Chaville realised that those were its hands. The demon looked badly beaten up, its throat already cut. Truly a different beast from the soldiers he had faced here so far.

The demon attempted to roar, but it coughed and spluttered. A truly pathetic creature, already broken. It ran at Chaville and swiped with one of its claws, but the paladin swung his sword upwards and lobbed its hand off.

It fell backwards, then awkwardly climbed to its feet. It swiped with its remaining claw, but Chaville cut it off too. He looked at the creature in disgust, as it lowered its head to try and gore him with its horns.

He dodged the attack and raised his sword once more, swinging hard and cutting its head from its body. It fell upon the bricks, dead.

Its death did not put Chaville at ease. If anything, he was more uneasy than ever. He started to piece together what had happened in his head. Alvaro had guided him here on the Blood Moon assassin's orders and the assassin was waiting inside. He had no doubt had a run-in with this demon already.

"Who awaits me?" asked Chaville under his

breath. "You will receive no mercy from me."

The paladin walked up the stairs, leaving the bodies of the demons to rot in the courtyard. Once he had dealt with the assassin, he would burn them on a pyre outside and reclaim this temple in the name of the True One.

Chaville reached for the doors and pushed them open. They were heavy, but they began to move, and the desecrated temple welcomed him inside, daring him to try and take it back from evil.

Chapter 11

Blood and Soul

Tarn stood in wait on a ceiling beam, leaning against the pillar. He was getting impatient waiting on the Outer Sentinel, but he had no doubt that he would be here. Each member was a formidable force, stronger than a dozen normal men, and the assassin would strike from a distance to ensure his own survival.

He listened intently for any sign of commotion in the courtyard. A Sentinel in a horde of demons would be incapable of keeping things quiet. Where the Sentinels charged head-on, the Blood Moon operated in the shadows. Honourable kills had little meaning, all that mattered was claiming the soul.

Tarn could see the moon hanging in the sky. He

kissed his ring and stared at it, humbled by its beauty. Only a true monarch would choose a resting place as grand as this. Somewhere that she could be admired across the entirety of the Outer World. If only everybody would pay her the respect that she so deserved.

Suddenly, the assassin's ears pricked up. He couldn't make out what it was, but something was happening in the courtyard. The Sentinel must have arrived.

Tarn reached into his pack and pulled out a small vial. He drenched a couple of throwing daggers in the green liquid that rested inside and waited, careful not to touch the toxin.

Minutes later, the doors of the church crept open. Tarn could see a shadowy figure in the doorway. The flesh golem stirred, having stood unmoving for as long as Tarn had been here.

Chaville raised his claymore and ran towards the golem. The hulking construct raised a fist and punched the nothingness in front of him, expelling sharp bones through the air. The paladin rolled aside, narrowly avoiding the unexpected attack.

He backed off slightly, waiting for the flesh golem to move. The brute started to walk towards him fearlessly. While not as heavy as the Fat Demon, the golem's weight was enough to shake the ceiling beams that Tarn stood upon.

The golem towered above the paladin, who dove between its legs. He spun around and slashed at its heels, but it barely noticed. The Outer Sentinel paused in surprise, clearly thinking whatever enchantments he had placed on his sword would have a greater effect. The flesh golem, however, was not a true demon. A foolish error for such an

esteemed figure to make.

It leapt aside, drawing back its fist. It slammed its knuckles at the Sentinel, who moved away just in time. When the golem raised its fist again, Tarn could see the crater it had left in the floor. Had the Sentinel been hit by that, Tarn's mission would have been a failure. He was counting on the man to be able to defeat this foe, not get crushed by it.

The battle continued for minutes, the paladin seemingly faring better. Suddenly, a sly kick from the golem and the man was on his back. The golem reached down and picked him up, about to break his back.

Tarn hurled one of his toxin-coated daggers at the golem's head, distracting it. Its grip loosened and Chaville wrestled free. He dropped to the ground and impaled the flesh golem's knee with his sword, swiftly leaping aside as the demon recoiled before dropping to its knees.

Chaville pulled his blade free then leapt up and cut the abomination's head from its body with a clean swing. As he turned to see where the dagger had come from, Tarn threw another. It passed by a small gap in the Sentinel's armour, grazing his neck.

The paladin fell to his knees and dropped his sword, no longer able to hold on. The fast-acting toxin spread throughout his whole body. He was numbed and helpless.

Tarn hopped onto a statue below and descended to the ground, satisfied that he had finally won. He would claim the man's soul for the Moonlight Queen.

"It...is you?" uttered Tarn, in shock. Up close he recognised the man's armour. It had to be the man he had seen briefly once before.

"Blood Moon..." muttered Chaville from the ground. Even with the grill from his helmet covering his face, Tarn knew the man had closed his eyes, realising what was about to happen to him. "Hurry up then, there's no point dragging it out."

Tarn dragged the armoured man up a small staircase and propped him against an altar, raising the grill. He gazed upon his target's face for the first time, wanting to look the Outer Sentinel in the eye before killing him.

"I recognise you," said the assassin.

"I cannot say the same for you," said the paladin, his attempts to raise his arms were in vain.

Tarn removed his mask, revealing his face. He had never shown his face before a kill, but he felt that he owed his saviour that much.

"Ah," said the paladin, letting out a grim laugh. "Castle Ouvergarde. You were the man in the cell that night."

"Yes," said Tarn. "You are the Outer Sentinel I was sent to kill."

"Isn't it funny how fate plays out?"

"For what it's worth, I did not know that you were Chaville."

"Had you known that, would it have changed a thing?"

"No," admitted Tarn. "It would not. That is the way it is for people like me. I do not have a choice in who I kill, nor would I want one. It makes things simpler in a sense."

"You always have the choice," said Chaville sternly. "What you mean is that you value your mission over the lives of the innocent. Is that not the case? At least admit it before I die. Give me an ounce of truth to take to the grave."

Tarn stared at the paladin intently. "I will restore the Moonlight Queen. Nothing will stand in my way. It may cost the lives of the innocent, but that is the price I am willing to pay. It is as simple as that."

Chaville started to laugh. There was nothing he could do in this situation but await his rapidly approaching fate. "Get on with it then."

"I am sorry that I have to do this. You can choose to believe me or not, but I have no desire to comfort my assigned targets."

"I believe you, but it does not matter to me. Either way, I am going to be murdered. I am going to receive a fate worse than death, my soul trapped in that ring on your finger. I wish that Alvaro had killed me on the bridge. I would even have preferred being crushed by the flesh golem's fist."

"Fate has simply played out in my favour this time."

"Wait," said Chaville, a flicker of light coming back to his eyes.

"It will do you no good to beg for your life. I thought that would be clear."

"It is not that," said the paladin. "However, I would like to make a small request, should you wish for a small piece of absolution."

"What is the request?"

"There is a tunnel to the south plagued by an army of golems. A few of them are demon golems and would be of great interest to the Outer Sentinels. Sir Florian knows where it is located. Send word however you please, use a civilian to pass the message along if need be."

Tarn understood. "I will make the request to them as a favour to you. If you would like to pray, I will grant you one more minute."

Chaville closed his eyes and began to pray, muttering under his breath. His arms were still immobile, unable to move far enough to clasp his hands together. He could not even bow his head anymore.

When the paladin opened his eyes, Tarn raised his sword and willed his ring to activate. "Thank you for saving me and thank you for saving the Outer World time and time again."

Chaville could not flinch as Tarn skewered him with his sword. The paladin died instantly and a whitish misty vapour escaped him, flowing into Tarn's ring. The ring slowly turned from a deep red to white, signifying that the assassin had completed his hunt. The Moonlight Queen would be pleased with him.

Tarn placed his mask back on his face and pulled the Sentinel's grill back down. In spite of everything, he could not leave the unfortunate man's body here. He could not leave it to be claimed by whatever demons remained nearby.

He grabbed Chaville's body by the arms and pulled him outside. He dragged him through the courtyard and into the trees lining the mountainside, far away from the path. It was a peaceful little spot, likely untouched by human feet for centuries. Somewhere the Outer Sentinel's body would not be disturbed.

The assassin spent hours digging in the rough soil, making a hole to bury the paladin. Once it was large enough to fit him, he rolled Chaville's corpse into the small pit.

Tarn grabbed his pack to see if there was anything that he could bring back to the shrine for the Blood Moon. No sense letting anything useful slip by. His respect for his mark only stretched so far.

"What have we here," Tarn muttered with a smile growing across his face and pulling out the golden mask with the butterfly design. "Joiselle, you naughty, naughty girl, did you try and claim my kill? It looks like I owe you another favour, Chaville."

Tarn hoped that she was not dead already, because he would ensure that she was excommunicated. Once she was no longer a Blood Moon, he was free to kill her himself without breaking any rules. He dug deeper into the paladin's pack, pulling out a small ring.

Having been captured and lost both his own mask and ring, Tarn would normally have had sympathy for a Blood Moon who had gotten themselves into an unfortunate situation like this. If only she had been more pleasant to him a few days ago, perhaps he would have returned them and wished her well. He chuckled and stashed them in his own pack, eager to return to the shrine. It had been quite the day and the reward was greater than he could have imagined.

As Tarn buried Chaville in the dirt, he sang the Ode to the Outer Sentinels.

For they are strong, for they have heart
Against the enemy, who tears apart
With evil sorcery, and wicked blood
That pours from the hells, the infernal flood

Slay them all, unleash your power
Our eternal souls, they will not devour
Raze their lairs, kill their kin
Nevermore, allow their sin
From us, the bounty plentiful
To you, our Outer Sentinel

The bittersweetness of this kill was hard to express, but Tarn was pleased that his good name would be restored in the Order of the Blood Moon. The humiliation of his recent capture would be overshadowed by achieving such a powerful soul as an offering for the Moonlight Queen.

He rose up and walked back into the courtyard and through the hole the clawed demon had torn in the side wall. He would take the more dangerous route down the mountainside in case Alvaro was waiting for him. The worm would not get his gold, he would not even get an extra silver penny from Tarn. Once he realised that, he would be keen to put a bolt in the assassin's skull.

Tarn carefully descended into the valley below, then leaping from a small cliff onto one of the roofs. Tarn slid down the side of the building, reaching the streets of Autun. It was a slow route, but he encountered no trouble. He walked through the town, spotting the remains of the Fat Demon. He laughed, knowing exactly how the beast had lost its life. Chaville was quite the hero. The assassin would send word to Sir Florian of the Outer Sentinels the next time he was close to a town that hadn't been overrun.

Tarn departed from Autun, never intending to return. He would await his crystal ring turning red, signalling a new task from the Moonlight Queen.

He would play his part in her resurrection, and he would take his place by her side as a most loyal servant.

Epilogue

Tarn sat at a table drinking mulled wine, awaiting the day he would be called to retrieve another soul for the Moonlight Queen. He stared at his ring, thinking of the souls that dwelled within. How many were there now? It had to be close to forty at this point.

Each kill had made the previous that much easier. So desensitised was Tarn that each time he recalled his earlier kills, he remembered them much differently than how they had occurred. The merchant minding his shop that he snuffed out from behind? Black market trader. The priest in the middle of his sermon? Accepting bribes to spread falsehoods. The Outer Sentinel a few years ago? There was no way that he was not a corrupt man. He must have been.

It was a strange phenomenon and he had felt it occur, but it slowly normalised inside his head. He had started to believe that it was the magic of the Moonlight Queen that had flowed through his ring, keeping him an effective assassin that did not suffer from pangs of guilt. No sooner had he started to dwell on the theory had the theory vanished from his mind as though it had never been there in the first place.

The assassin finished his drink and set his cup on the table then took to pacing the halls. It had been three days since he completed his last bounty and he had come to loathe the unproductive downtime between jobs. He was restless and wanted to return to the thrill of the hunt. It was the only thing that made him feel normal, yet it was the most abnormal thing about him.

He walked into the main chamber where three of his fellow assassins were discussing the findings of their latest scrying ritual. By the sounds of things, they had learned little and would be trying again in a few hours in the hope of their target being somewhere more identifiable.

Tarn kneeled at the foot of the Moonlight Queen's statue, a near identical statue to the one in the Rochian shrine in the pine forest. He prayed to the Queen, asking her to send him his next mission. Was he not faithful? Had he not claimed each soul required of him over the years?

As if to answer his prayer, his ring started to glow red. Tarn jumped to his feet and called over the other assassins, Guion was amongst them. Tarn waited for them to assume their positions, and then he began his chant.

His ring shone and the other assassins joined

in. Tarn's eyes glowed red and he levitated above the stone floor to face the Queen's statue. As its crystal glowed, Tarn's eyes were sent across the realms, and he could see through the eyes of another as though it were a window.

He was notably shorter than before, leaning on a fence beside a beautiful green field. A horse stood in front of him, dragging a hoof softly along the ground, and he reached out a delicate hand to stroke it. Was this a woman's body? It must be. No man would have skin that pure and soft, not even the most pampered of the most pampered nobles.

The woman glanced towards a city a short way down the road. It was surrounded by walls that reached high, but towers within the city reached even higher. Tarn recognised it, but it was a dangerous place. One that was dreaded far and wide these days.

Tarn brought himself back to the shrine, and he returned to the ground.

"Where was that, Master Tarn?" asked one of the assassins.

Tarn caught his breath. "The target is a woman, I'm certain of it. She was in a field outside of Altburg stroking a horse. A mare, I believe."

"Altburg?" asked the assassin. "Who would dare go there in a time like this? I heard that even looters avoid it like the plague. Considering it recovered from a plague only years ago, that's not insignificant. There are more demons in that city than there are people and by no small number, at that."

"Yes, you're right of course," replied Tarn. "If the woman is smart, she would stay away from that hellscape. Perhaps she has another reason for being there, but it does not matter. I will find her."

Guion, quiet as ever, finally piped up. "I'm sure you have heard what happened to our fellow assassin, Amiens, when he was tasked with a bounty in the city?"

Tarn and the other Blood Moon assassins all nodded solemnly. It had been a tough couple of years for the Order of the Blood Moon, with many members failing their tasks. Too many of their rings had been lost in irretrievable places. Hundreds of souls wasted, all trapped eternally, never to be gifted to the queen. Never to help restore her to life and bring her down from her orbital burial ground.

"A tragedy it is, Guion. Perhaps if he had wandered into a pine forest he would have fared better," jabbed Tarn.

Guion scowled behind his mask and pointed his right arm at Tarn. "I am giving you a fair warning. You still do not believe that I knew nothing of the sylvans? Joiselle was your enemy, not me. She is no longer a problem as I'm sure you're all too aware."

Tarn stared at Guion's outstretched arm, quietly gleeful that there was no hand attached to it. "Apologies, brother," he said to his comrade.

Guion nodded in acceptance of the apology. Not wanting to break the rules of the order, Tarn had refrained from orchestrating Guion's death, but had managed to lead the quiet assassin into an unfortunate accident. Guion was of course suspicious of Tarn's involvement, as were a lot of their fellow assassins, but the high council had cleared him of all wrongdoing.

It had certainly been an eventful few years for

Tarn and his skills had only grown. Never since had he been captured by an enemy. Never since did he have trouble locating a target. No, he was more skilled than ever, and his rank had increased substantially. It felt good to be both respected and feared by his peers.

Tarn wandered to the back rooms and gathered his gear, readying himself for an imminent departure. It was a few weeks on the road to reach Altburg from here in the Kingdom of Kalmere, but he had to find the woman with the horse. The Moonlight Queen demanded it.

Other Books by Jordan Allen

Mutagenesis: The New World (2021)

A post-apocalyptic sci-fi novel set in Texas decades after hordes of mutants wiped out civilisation. It's a tale of survival, adventure and coming to terms with misfortune.

Hollow Kingdom (2023)

The first book in the dark fantasy series, the Hollow Realms. A sword and sorcery tale of a prince trying to reclaim his kingdom and solve the mystery of his father and brother's fates.

Ashes of the Necropolis (2023)

The second book in the dark fantasy series, the Hollow Realms. A mercenary seeks his missing companions in a city filled with the undead and at the mercy of a wicked lich.

www.ingramcontent.com/pod-product-compliance
Lightning Source LLC
Chambersburg PA
CBHW072356190626
46811CB00019B/1091